CHARLES EINSTEIN

NO TIME AT ALL

SIMON AND SCHUSTER   NEW YORK   1957

All sorts of unexpected misadventures are possible in commercial aviation, and truth is often stranger than fiction. As a matter of fact at least one commercial airliner in recent history actually experienced the same breakdown as that suffered by the plane in this story.

Nonetheless, this book is strictly a work of fiction. Perhaps it is even more so than most novels, since it deals almost exclusively with people affected by a dramatic situation in the air—but not directly, and not in actual peril of their own lives. A writer can only guess what their reactions might be. There is no standard operating procedure at all.

In other words, an accident like the one herein described is possible, having in fact already happened. But the situations and people in this story are constructed from imagination. There is no airline known as Coastal, and any similarity between names of persons in the book and real persons who have been involved in similar circumstances is completely coincidental.

Finally, flying is a form of transportation which actually has an extra measure of safety over all others. Commercial airlines, in the face of the newspaper space any air crash receives, have dedicated themselves to the mechanics of safety. No private automobile begins to receive so frequent and thorough a check as the commercial airliner. Yet flying is the only form of transportation that man is not equipped to accomplish unaided. He can walk and he can swim, but he cannot fly. Thus, instinctively, when he deals directly or indirectly with matters of the air he finds them less familiar, and so he himself becomes a little less predictable.

SCOTTSDALE, ARIZONA, 1957 —C.E.

CONTENTS

NO TIME AT ALL

part one: THE NEWS

To MILLIONS of Americans who would hear
about her in the next few hours, she would be described
erroneously as a Super Constellation and as a DC-7, and by
one enthusiastic radio announcer in Des Moines, Iowa, even
as a DC-7 Constellation. She would be described as a giant
four-motored air liner, and purists would take the time to

point out that airplanes have engines, not motors. To her crew she was known in unlovely language as the Everyinch, because, flying the Miami–New York run in late summer, she tended to light passenger bookings, and so this one ship of the line had had all but twenty passenger seats ripped out and the rear fuselage turned over to cargo—thus the airline sought to make every inch pay.

But most generally she was known as Coastal 214.

Coastal was the name of the airline and 214 the number of the flight, northbound from Miami to New York nonstop, away from the ramp one minute late, at 7:31 P.M., held at the runway while two big babies, a National 6B and an Eastern Connie, came down in the lowering murk and thin twilight rain that advertised the Caribbean touch of the season's first hurricane.

At 7:36, Coastal 214 was airborne with flight plan filed for instrument procedure above the clouds at 17,000 feet. Contact was made with Air Traffic Control according to routine shortly after 1,000 feet. At 7:49, already in cloud, the plane passed over West Palm Beach and now was over the Atlantic Ocean. Because her route lay off the eastern coast of the United States, the Everyinch was favored with an additional safety factor. No fewer than half a dozen radar screens, including the military, watched her. Her next radio check was scheduled for 8:04 P.M., into ATC at Jacksonville, which also was equipped with radar.

But Coastal 214 did not report.

AT THIS SAME TIME, a curious, half-humorous incident was taking place at the Kansas City Municipal Airport. An elderly man named William Goldstone was awaiting the plane from the West that would take him to New York. When the plane came in and taxied to a stop at the apron, the pilot kept his engines running for some six or seven minutes. The backwash from the propellers made it impossible to wheel the passenger ramp up to the plane. Finally, the pilot cut the engines, and among the passengers who got off was one extremely white-faced man.

William Goldstone, standing there at the gate, said to him, "Was there any trouble?"

"Trouble?" the man said. "Trouble? Just an engine quit on us, that's all." He swallowed. "Mister, I was going to New Orleans, but no more. Where are we? Kansas City? I'll stay here. The hell with this plane. The hell with flying." His talk was disjointed. "I need a drink. You look like a nice fella. Can you get a drink here? Come on. I'll buy you one."

William Goldstone shook his head. "No," he said. "I don't want to lose my place on line."

"What are you going to do?" the other man said. "Get on that plane? After what I just told you?"

William Goldstone shrugged. "If the pilot gets on," he said, "I will too."

And he smiled, William Goldstone did; he did not tell this frightened man that his own son Marvin was a flight engineer, destined possibly someday to be a full-fledged captain, for one of the nation's biggest airlines. William Goldstone had heard the facts time and again from his own son. He knew, therefore, how safe it is to fly.

THE FIRST REALIZATION that Coastal 214 was in trouble —the first inkling for those on the ground, at any rate—

brought with it a delicate but meaningful shift in terminology. Nobody again tonight would refer to the Everyinch as "she."

ATC Jacksonville, with jurisdiction for this leg, had Oscar Meggs on the control desk. He looked at the clock on the wall, then at the watch on his wrist, then at the flight plan before him. He was a thin, leathery-faced young man, brittle and impatient in character, which in its way made him good at his job. Ed Benson, older and heavier and with more patience per extra pound than Meggs, walked from the radar cubicle at the end of the room and picked up an idle headset, holding it momentarily to one ear. "Static, static, and then static. Ee-ya, it goes. Squeee."

"Cut it out," Meggs said to him.

"Oh, it'll get worse," Benson said. "Wait till your hurricane starts up the coast. Even if she stays out to sea, what do you have for four hundred miles around? Ee-ya. Squeee. We had a place in Daytona Beach, here, eighteen, twenty years ago. That's when the hurricanes were still belting Florida for the main fall. We had one baby come in . . ."

"He's late," Meggs cut in: the word "he."

"Who's late?"

"Coastal 214."

"What time is it now?" Benson said, and looked at the clock. "Eight-oh-eight. When's he due?"

"Oh-four," Meggs said, and shook his head. He did not like to talk while wearing a headset. Now he reached for the table microphone and switched on the room amplifier so he could work for a time without headphones.

"Well, he's there," Benson said easily. He too was good at his work. "He's on the screen inside."

"I'm going to ask him," Meggs said.

"Really? What for? He's not that late."

"Five minutes now. Going on six."

"Large deal. Maybe he's got some lightning around him. Doesn't want to talk right now."

"Weather didn't say any lightning out there."

"You know Weather. They're lucky they know a hurricane's coming."

Meggs looked at the older man for a minute. Then he said into the microphone, his voice Southern and polite, masking any tension or even any impatience he might be feeling, "Coastal 214, this is Jacksonville. Will you report, please?"

Static crumpled the air. The two men waited. Then, seeming to be inside the static, but clearly understandable withal, a voice said, "Jacksonville, this is Coastal . . ." Meggs's shoulders lowered, then raised at the next words: ". . . 73, off at oh-seven, climbing to ten thousand en route for New Orleans over Lake City, Perry, Port St. Joe and the Gulf. I should be in clouds before two thousand."

Meggs nodded and leaned to his microphone. "You check again at eight-thirty, 73. Barometer two-nine-point-five-oh. You hear that all right?"

"Loud and clear. 73."

"73; Jacksonville. You hear us call Coastal 214—two-one-four—just before now?"

"We weren't over to you from the airport till just when we called in," 73 said.

"Now, Coastal 214, you hear me now?" Meggs said.

"This is 73. I heard that all right," the voice in the air said, after a crackling pause. "Can't you get him?"

"Not just now, but we've got him on our screen," Meggs

5

said calmly. "I believe he may be reporting any minute now. He may have let the time slide by a little. Maybe he's encountered turbulence. Maybe a little electricity."

"What's today?" 73 said. "Tuesday? Hell, that 214's the Everyinch. He's the one carries live goats. Ain't nothing ever going to happen to him."

"All right," Meggs said into the microphone. He looked over at Benson. "You sure you got him?"

Benson had gone back to the radar screen, and now he stared at it as though he wished he could remove it from its moorings and hold it up the way doctors scrutinize X rays. "Now, don't tell me that's not a plane," he said, and fingered a small, irregular blob almost accusingly. "I've seen clouds and I've seen planes, and that's a plane."

"Is it him? You've got more than one plane."

"Over here?" Benson jabbed with his finger. "Who else would it be?"

The amplifier said, "Special 188. Jacksonville, this is Special 188."

Special 188 was a chartered army plane, also flying Miami to New York. It had taken off minutes after the Coastal flight.

Meggs said into the microphone, "Jacksonville to 188. Barometer twenty-nine-point-five-oh. What's your altitude?" He was looking at 188's flight plan.

One eighty-eight gave him his compass heading, air speed, and altitude. Meggs said, "All right." Then: "Wait a minute." He called in to Benson, "You should have that 188 there too."

"Moving up on him and a little to his right," Benson said. "Yuh. Two of them."

6

Meggs decided to order a change. He said into the microphone, "One eighty-eight, continue to climb to eighteen thousand feet. One-eight. Do you read that?"

"I'm over clouds now," 188 said.

"Climb steadily to eighteen thousand regardless," Meggs said.

"One eighty-eight."

"Your next check is eight-fifty."

"Thank you and good night for now."

Meggs set the microphone down, then picked it up again and said, "Coastal 214, we are trying to identify you. This is Jacksonville."

In the static, a voice said, "Coastal 73. How long is he . . ."

"Will you stay off for now, 73, please?" Meggs said. His voice retained the same measure of control as before. "Coastal 214, this is Jacksonville."

"Give me that flight plan," Benson said, coming over to the shelf-desk where Meggs was at work. "Let me check it with Miami." He vanished into an adjacent room. A moment later he stuck his head through the door. He looked at the clock, then said: "No. That's confirmed."

"Look at that screen for me again, will you?" Meggs said. "I'm going to keep trying him. Coastal 214, this is Jacksonville . . ."

Benson peered at the screen. "That's got to be a plane."

"Is it him?"

"Sure it's him. Right over here from this other one. What are we supposed to have here? Two planes. What have we got? Two planes."

"You're sure?"

"Sure I'm sure. He's right where he's supposed to be. Besides—" Benson moistened his lips—"if it isn't him, who is it?"

"I don't know," Meggs said. "I don't know." It occurred to him quite suddenly that in four years at this job he had never once run into this situation before. "What do we do?"

"Let me take a headset," Benson said, "and try some different wave lengths." He did so. After three minutes or so he took off the headset and said, "He may be keeping silence."

"For extreme thunderheads or something like that," Meggs said. "And we don't know of any out there. And besides, if he hit that kind of unexpected weather, he would've let us know it. Now, wouldn't he?"

"You'd think so," Benson said. "But you heard what his friend said. He's flying goats. Maybe he thinks it don't count."

"Maybe he can hear us but we can't hear him," Meggs said.

Benson nodded. "It's just possible. Try him again."

Meggs spread his palms. "Coastal 214, this is Jacksonville. Can you hear me? Coastal 214 . . ."

For a handful of minutes more, they stayed that way, Meggs at the microphone and the older man, his face a deep red against the open-throated blue gingham shirt he wore, peering at the radar screen. Then Benson turned his head. "Tell him what I tell you. Coastal 214, this is Jacksonville . . ."

Meggs said into his microphone, "Coastal 214, this is Jacksonville."

"We do not hear you but if you can hear us . . ."

"We do not hear you but if you can hear us . . ."

". . . we are trying to establish a radar fix. Make a right turn."

". . . we are trying to establish a radar fix. Make a right turn." Meggs took his hand away from the microphone and said to Benson, "What about that other plane? The special?"

"Don't worry about it," Benson said. "He's got to be up above him. Now. Right turn at ninety degrees and continue on that heading."

"Ninety degrees right turn," Meggs said into the microphone, "and continue on that heading." He had obeyed Benson's instructions down even to inflection of words.

"Now let's watch him," Benson said, and Meggs leaned back, trying to see the screen from there.

"What's happening?" the younger man said.

"Far as I can tell, nothing," Benson said. "Give him a chance, now. Repeat the thing and tell him we'll give him a minute or two. He may be in the middle of something."

Meggs relayed the word again.

For two minutes, Benson stared at the screen. At last, he looked up and said, "If it's him, his radios are out."

"*If* it's him?" Meggs said quickly. "A minute ago you said you were positive it *was* him."

"Of course it's him," Benson said. "But his radio's out, that's all."

"I don't believe it," Meggs said. "He wouldn't be up there."

"What?"

"He's not that far out of Miami. If something like that happened, he would have turned around and gone back. First thing."

"And land where?"

"Miami." He began to think about it. "Or . . ."

"Yeah," Benson said. "Or."

"Well, he's got instruments," Meggs said. "Even if he doesn't have radio contact. Hey, I just thought of something."

"What's that?"

"You suppose the trouble could be here? Something wrong with *our* set?"

A voice in the static said, "Jacksonville, Coastal 73."

"This is Jacksonville," Meggs said automatically into the microphone.

"Raise him yet?"

"Not yet."

"Oh-oh," 73 said, then gave his checkpoint report.

"Well," Benson said. He nodded dourly at Meggs. "You still think *our* radio is no good?"

"Well, I never heard of anything like this," Meggs said. "Your radio goes out—all nine of them, or however many he's got—and your instruments are fine, your plane is still flying . . ."

"Who told you that?"

"The plane's still flying? You did. Off the radar. You said . . ."

Benson put up a hand. "Who told you his instruments were working?"

Meggs blinked. "His radio and electrical systems both out? Together?"

"The only case of that kind I know of," Benson said, "was that plane from Boston to New York. Not too long ago. Winter of '55–'56. And that's exactly what happened to him."

Meggs thought for a moment. "Boston to New York is one thing. Anyway, that guy could get down under the clouds and see. I remember it."

"This guy can too."

They were talking about it as if it were an accomplished truth.

"But he's got a much longer flight," Meggs said.

"And that much bigger a fuel load to make a landing that much tougher if he didn't stay up for a while to burn it off."

"He could jettison some fuel," Meggs said. He laughed hoarsely. "If his electricity and his radios are both off, he can get rid of gasoline in perfect safety."

"Yup," Benson said. "Then what does he use to fly with if he can't locate a field?"

They were guessing now. They were trying to think. They were helpless, and it occurred to both of them at the same time that it would be wholly in order at this point to let others in on their helplessness.

"Let's get on the teletype," Benson said. "We'll have to tell Miami and New York."

"And Washington," Meggs said.

Aside from the ATC communications network, operated under the CAA, Coastal Airlines had its own teletype system, of course. So far tonight, its action had been sporadic, as it always was at the New York end. Coastal was franchised only into LaGuardia, and there only for Miami service, a matter that held occasional fascination for a young man named Willard Trace. Trace was, at the age of twenty-three, in charge of the Operations Office for Coastal at the New York airport. The mathematics and the politics that went into route planning and grants for the different airlines intrigued him—the way, for example, TWA flew the Albuquerque-Tucson route but could not book any passengers between those two cities, because of a competing local airline. Now, to take a more germane example, Willard Trace knew that Coastal was trying every string in its bow to add Washington nonstop service from New York and Miami to its schedules. As of the moment, the Miami–New York nonstop was its only approved entry into New York. There were endless details. Delivery of DC-7 equipment for the airline was close at hand, but to put the 7's into New York–Miami service would require facilities not at LaGuardia but at Idlewild, because of the longer runways at the latter. It was all right to land a 7 at LaGuardia, when most of its fuel weight had been burned up, but you could not take off with a full passenger and fuel load from the same field. Willard Trace did not know the exact weight/footage requirements, but somebody had told him it would be all right to take off in a 7 from La-Guardia only with practically all seats empty.

And as of this moment, one of the things that fascinated him most was that while the Miami–New York service was only a small part of the Coastal scheduling (its main service was concentrated in the Miami-Cincinnati-Dallas triangle), the line's head offices were here in New York. It made no sense, but there it was.

And to be chief of the LaGuardia Operations Office for the airline at the age of twenty-three was hardly the honor such a title betokened. There was nothing to do but watch the teletype and make sure the weather advices were readied for the flight crews; to clock flights and their crews; to invoice gasoline and catered flight-meal consumption; to clock flights and their crews in and out; and—for the most part, and this was the truth of it—run errands. Freight and Ticketing had their own offices. All Willard

Trace had to do was sit around, alone, in Operations, and that was what he was doing now.

He was, finally, estimably suited to his job that required little or no talent. In fact, it was his older brother, Mike Trace, who had got him the job to begin with. Mike was ten years older than Willard, and Mike was a pilot for Coastal. Tonight, he was flying 214, the Everyinch, up from Miami.

The teletype had had only two messages that dealt with 214 so far. One of them, timed off at 7:40 P.M., said:

NY 214 OFF AT 36. MF 740P XLDDDD

"MF" stood for Miami, Florida, and here designated the sender of the message.

Then, at 8:07:

NY CARGO 214 HAS CRATED DOG. DO NOT (REPEAT NOT) TAKE FROM CRATE. DOG BITES. MF 807P RLHHH

Cargo would get that message in its own office at La-Guardia, and there would be the usual serio-comic nodding of heads among the freight personnel, because the Every-inch inevitably would show up with at least four crated dogs, and no one would know which the biter was. The theory of most freight handlers was that out of every group of four crated dogs, the second smallest dog would be the one that bit.

The teletype was on its best behavior tonight; especially with the weather as it was all the way up the coast. Ceiling at LaGuardia now was nearly two thousand feet, with a light rain, but it was going to get worse, just as the weather was going to get worse. Weather. *Sunspots*, Willard Trace said to himself. People were always talking about what sunspots did to radio reception. They ought to see a teletype circuit gone blooey.

Two bells sounded on the teletype, cutting the silence now, and Willard Trace put aside his copy of *Flaming Detective* and went to the machine at once. Two bells usually signified a message that required an answer, though the same signal could be applied to any message that for any reason stood out from the strictly routine. Willard Trace moved quickly to the machine, not out of any idealistic stirrings but because there was the likelihood that an answer would be needed, and it gave him a sense of power to show other stations along the line how quickly New York responded. (Actually, when he did reply to a message, it was almost invariably merely to acknowledge it, with the symbol KK. Then he would have to get instructions from elsewhere in order to punch out the ensuing reply.)

As he neared the teletype, Willard Trace looked at the clock on the wall. He would compare it to the time-off on the message, just to see how clocks in different offices along the line compared. Not that it made any difference. Nothing, in the attention to detail that Willard Trace displayed so assiduously from time to time, made much difference.

The clock said 8:39.

Trace watched the message as the keys sprang to and spelled it out.

NY THIS MF. FYI ATC JAX SEZ 214 27 (REPEAT 27)
MINS OVERDUE REPORTING

Willard Trace felt his throat come up, growing tighter and larger, as it must be with the twine-winding of a baseball at the factory. His first thought, in truth, was that he was being told about a plane in trouble and was expected to do something about it. He had never experienced anything like this before. In all the time he had spent at La-Guardia, he had seen only one accident, when a nose wheel gave, and it was not much of an accident.

His second thought, and only his second, was that his brother was flying Coastal 214.

But a third thought came along, almost instantly, to cushion and lessen the second—that third thought was that 214 was all right: the teletype machine was not stopping; there was more to it; the machine pulsed a few times and started on another word, so it would turn out that 214, having been 27 minutes overdue, had at that point finally reported.

The message continued:

THERE   AND   UNABLE
CONTACT RADIOWISE. BUT

(*But what?* Trace asked himself.)

BELIEVE   CAN   IDENTIFY
RADARWISE AND RADAR HERE SAYS ALSO BELIEVE
SAME. APPEARS

Again the teletype paused and pulsed. Willard Trace swallowed. His eyes were large.

The message took up again.

BE ON COURSE. POSSIBLY MAIN-
TAINING RADIO SILENCE SOME REASON PROBABLY
WEATHER. MF 841P DLLLL

Willard Trace looked around the room. He looked at the
clock on the wall: 8:41. The clocks were doing fine.

Automatically, he pressed the lever on the teletype to
the "Send" position and typed out:

MF JJ ///// KK NY 84

He looked at the clock.

2P NY

Now what was he supposed to do?

Ordinarily, he could call the Operations Officer in Manhattan, but it was nighttime now. The Operations Officer
had a home phone number. He was, Trace knew, a vice-
president of the airline. What was his name? Trace never
had had reason to need this name before. The name . . .
was it Kent? Where was the book giving the home phone
numbers; or would it be buried on the clipboard instead?

Willard Trace looked around the room, and his eyes did
not tell him where the number would be. He grasped the
telephone—something to do—and dialed.

A terribly cheerful voice at the other end answered:
"A-MER-ican Airlines! Reservations-are-busy-will-you-
wait?"

Trace had misdialed. At the same time, he felt a sense
of irritation. All the airlines did this. When they said "Reservations" they meant "Reservations—Information—Com-

16

plaints—everything." But this was not apparent to the slob who called in to see if his mother-in-law's plane would be on time. And if he tried to say he didn't want a reservation, but, instead, information, he found himself talking to an empty line, the slob did.

But Willard Trace, no slob he, was on the inside. He was a part of the mystic inner circle of the airlines, not apart from it. The next time he dialed correctly, getting Coastal's cargo office at LaGuardia.

A voice answered. "Harrison. Coastal Cargo."

"Trace in Operations," Willard Trace said. "Did you see the message?"

"What message?"

"On the teletype. Just came in." Trace wet his lips. "Two bells."

"What does it say?"

Willard Trace paused for a moment before replying. Then he said, "Plane in trouble."

"What kind of trouble?"

"Plane," Trace said dimly.

"One of ours?" the voice named Harrison said. It was another needless question. "Wait a minute." Harrison was gone for a moment, then returned. "Well?"

"Did you read it?"

"Uh-huh."

"What do you think?"

"I don't know. Probably what it says. Weather."

"It doesn't sound that way to me."

"There's a hurricane coming this way, buster."

"It doesn't sound that way to me," Willard Trace said again.

"Oh," Harrison said. "Who are you?"

"What do you mean, who am I?"

"You sounded so positive," Harrison said. "I thought you were General Nathan Twining or somebody."

"Listen . . ." Trace said. His voice had taken on a tinge of the dramatic.

Harrison said, "I'm listening."

Trace waited for a moment. Then he said, "You know who's flying that plane?"

"No."

"My brother."

"Oh," Harrison said. "He is?"

"Yes," Willard Trace said. "What are we going to do?"

"Well, I don't know what we can do," Harrison said. "Do you?"

"I thought maybe I ought to phone the Operations Officer," Trace said. "I never had a wreck." It was a pardonable first person that he employed.

"Neither did I," Harrison said.

"We ought to do something," Trace said.

"Okay," Harrison said. "You name it."

"Well, I thought I'd phone the Operations Officer," Trace said again. "Maybe he'd know what to do."

"Yuh," Harrison said. Then he thought of something. "Hell. *You're* the Operations Officer."

"No," Willard Trace said. "I'm in charge of the Operations Office at one airport. You understand? Just here. That doesn't make me Operations Officer for the whole she-bang."

"It's confusing," Harrison said. "Well, damn, *I* don't know. Who *is* the Operations Officer?"

"I don't know," Trace said. "I thought it was Kent."

"Kent? He's a big muck-a-muck. He's vice-president."

"But *the* Operations Officer," Trace said.

"Well, I don't know," Harrison said. "All we handle at this end is coffins and lobsters. What can I tell you?"

"It's Kent," Willard Trace said.

"Okay," Harrison said. "It's Kent. Call him and tell him."

"I'm looking for his number."

"Well," Harrison said, "you'll find it there sooner'n we'll find it here."

"Could it be weather?"

"Dunno. What's the weather been down there?"

"Florida?"

"Uh-huh. Miami."

"Somebody said raining."

"Well, there you are," Harrison said, as if that proved something.

"I think it's raining, anyway."

"It's a hurricane coming that way, isn't it?"

"I could check the weather advisory."

"Uh-huh. Anyway. What the hell? They can see him on radar."

"They *think* they can."

"Your brother Mike's a good pilot," Harrison said. "Ain't nothing going to happen to him."

"I wonder about Emmy," Trace said.

"Who?"

"Emmy."

"Who's that?"

"Mike's girl," Trace said. "How is she going to take something like this?"

"Stop it, will you?" Harrison said over the phone. "Snap off it, kid. You talk like he's already . . . what are you talking that way for?"

"It's all right," Willard Trace said.

"Ain't your brother married?" Harrison said. "What's this, his girl?"

"He used to be married," Willard Trace said.

"Oh," Harrison said.

"He's not any more," Trace said. Then he said again, "It's all right." Already the great and peaceful wounds of martyrdom had begun to settle on him. *Lost flyer's brother. Clung to his post.* "I'll stay here."

"Where would you go if you didn't?" Harrison asked.

"You don't understand," Trace said. "You just don't understand. If you had a brother who . . ."

"All right, kid, all right, all right," Harrison said. He paused for a moment. "We'll keep in touch. Okay?"

"Sure," Trace said.

"Fine," Harrison said. Then he hung up the phone.

Willard Trace looked around the room. Slowly, he set the telephone receiver back in place upon its cradle. He thought for a moment. Then a smile came to his face—the sad, set smile of certain doom.

Yet it was a brave smile.

He knew what he had to do.

He picked up the phone again. This time he dialed Emmy's number.

No," Ben Gammon, the newspaperman, said. "I'm not going to quote you poetry. You think because I can't fly an airplane I have to be able to quote poetry. There's something psychiatric in all of that. Those who can, do. Those who can't, quote."

Emmy Verdon came out of the cubbyhole that served as a kitchen in her Manhattan apartment. She wore a half-apron over a blue cotton dress. The blue went surprisingly well with the summer tan upon her face and her throat and her legs. She was a tall girl, black-haired, and she had the face of a country girl, the cheeks perhaps too full to make it a perfect face. Tall, and there was an adjective that could be applied to this kind of tallness in a woman, except that it was a much misinterpreted word—the adjective was *leggy*. Whatever it was, she knew it, and she knew what it could do. She wore a little lipstick, but no other make-up at all.

She said, "I thought all college men knew poetry."

"I'm not exactly a college man," Ben Gammon said.

"No?"

"Not exactly, no."

"You have a diploma, don't you?"

"My mother has it."

"Well?"

"It's a Ph.B. from the University of Chicago."

"Isn't that a degree?"

"To a degree," Gammon said, and nodded solemnly. "Most people wouldn't know the difference. That's most people, I say. But you spotted it at once."

"I did?"

"Yes," he said. "You asked me to quote poetry and I told you I didn't know any poetry."

"Well," she said. "All right." She turned and went back to the kitchen, drying her hands on her apron as she went. It was an instinctive gesture more than anything else, because the next moment her hands were back in the soapy dishwater in the sink. "I just thought you might know some," she called through the open door. "Some Swinburne, maybe."

"Algernon Charles?"

"Algernon Charles," she said.

"1837–1909," he said.

"What's that?"

"1837–1909," he said. "His dates. My God. He lived to be seventy-two."

"Is that so surprising?"

"Sure it is. What was the life expectancy in those days? Thirty-three years. Something like that."

"No," Emmy said from the kitchen. "That was in Rome. The Roman Empire. Way back when."

"You doubt my word," he said, loudly and comfortably, lying on the couch and talking at the ceiling. "The lady doubts the man's word."

"Not at all," she said from the kitchen. "How can you say I doubt your word? Did I say anything when you said his dates were whatever they were?"

"1837–1909, or so I do believe," he said. "No, come to think of it, you didn't. You trust me implicitly. Do you trust your flyboy the same?"

"Listen," Emmy said, coming to the door of the kitchen, "stop talking about my flyboy."

"But you're his girl," Ben Gammon said to her. "His lady fair."

"If I were," Emmy said, "you wouldn't be here eating my meat loaf and lying on my couch."

"I wouldn't?"

"No. You wouldn't."

"He's away," Gammon said. "That's the thing of it. While the Coastal Airline Pilot's Away, the Mouse Will . . ."

"He's not away," she said. "If you're interested, and you seem to be, he's flying in tonight."

"Ah," Gammon said, "and he can see us now. He's watching us on his little patented device, up there high above the clouds, watching us, everything we do."

"Stop it," she said.

"He asked you to marry him," Gammon said.

"I didn't say yes."

"Not yet, you didn't. You will."

"Really?"

"Yuh. Really." He crossed his feet, lying there on the couch. "It appeals to your sense of danger. Peril. Pilot in the uncharted skies."

Emmy went back to the dishes. "You're very sure, aren't you?"

"Yes, ma'm."

"Then why did you bother to come tonight?" Her voice was light, but the question was the question none the less.

"A good question," he said now. "Why did I bother to come?"

"Well?"

"You invited me."

"Doesn't that mean anything?"

"With most people, yes," Gammon said. "With me, no."

"Oh," Emmy said. "I see. Algernon Charles Swinburne is a special case all by himself."

"That's right," Gammon said. "Right you are."

"And why?"

"Because." Gammon's hand felt for a cigarette on the coffee table. "I'm never sure when pretty ladies invite me. I mean, sure of what's behind it all. Sometimes I think I make things so tough for everybody that what really happens is I invite myself. I'm that kind. Obnoxious. Real obnoxious. Like your flyboy's brother who keeps calling up when the flyboy's out of town. Just to check up on you. What's his name?"

"Willard," Emmy said.

"Willard Trace," Ben Gammon said.

"And?" Emmy said.

"And Willard is a good name for this," Gammon said. "Well. As I say. Obnoxious. It's easier to invite me than to not invite me. You know?"

"No," she said. "I don't know."

"The meat loaf was spectacular."

"Thank you."

"You cook so good for the flyboy?"

"Shut up," Emmy said. She had known Mike Trace, the pilot, for more than a year now; Ben Gammon she had known for only two months or so, and perhaps the most notable facet in this triangle—if triangle it truthfully was —was Emmy Verdon's curiosity. At the age of twenty-four she had the woman's wisdom that said that love was not, to put it into a phrase, like the movies. Love was a process of becoming accustomed. The words in the songs, the flashes in the night, the distant drums on the distant shores . . . all these, she supposed, were possible. At least they served as an estimable excuse. But after these many months, she was used to Mike Trace, and fonder of him for it. Perhaps Gammon was right when he said she would marry him. And yet, ridiculously enough, unless you stopped to think it all the way through, Gammon's being right could be what would stop her.

She was curious; curious now about Gammon. In the purer sense of the word, she did not particularly like him, but that was a deceptive way to put it, because it was not that simple. It was easy to say you loved someone but did not like him—almost too easy—but if a situation like that was true it deserved a closer inspection and a deeper explanation. Emmy did not like Gammon for his tongue, and from time to time she found herself disliking him for his insight; the one was sharper than the other. He was thirty-two, a year younger than Mike Trace. He had never been married; Trace had, briefly, in the past of five or six or seven years ago. Ben did not carry in his job, as a reporter for a wire service, the dramatic personal responsibility that Mike Trace carried on his shoulders as a ranking captain of the line for an air carrier. In picking reporters, a wire service did not look for soundness and coolness of judgment the way an airline looked for these things in a prospective pilot. Sometimes soundness and coolness of judgment were what a wire service got from its reporters, but then it was getting a little more than it deserved.

And yet, with all of this, it was not safe for Emmy to say to herself that Mike Trace was a more mature individual than Ben Gammon, even though by every yardstick he should be so. Nor even could she—herself, alone—vow that Trace was more exciting as a man, though by all odds he was the more handsome of the two. Gammon was lean, and pale of face, with deepset eyes. Already, the hair was beginning to recede from his forehead. There was nothing really wrong with him physically—he had told her this—

yet he took both kinds of the popular pills, the ones that elated and the ones that sedated.

"Like Alice in Wonderland," he told her. "One side of the mushroom makes you grow tall and the other side makes your chin hit against your foot."

"I wonder what an analyst would say about you," she had said.

"Analysts," he replied. "I feel sorry for them."

"Why? *You* feel sorry for *them?*"

"Sure. Years they went, yelling and yammering about how mental illness was the same thing—disease, of its own kind—as physical illness. Then—all of a sudden—*whap.* They got the pill for everything. People suddenly agree. Mental illness *can* be treated the same as physical illness. Treat it with a pill. Same way. So all of a sudden what? All of a sudden the analysts start going out of business, that's what. Ah. What do they do now? They have their annual convention at Atlantic City or someplace and they draft a Resolution. Capital *R.* The pills are not the answer, say they. Sow the wind, and ye shall . . ."

"So," Emmy had put in. "You think the pills are the answer."

"I didn't say that. All I know for sure is the pills are cheaper. Eleven cents a pop."

Still she had also seen him, only recently, go a solid week without the pills, and it had made no difference to him.

"Why don't you give them up altogether?" she asked.

"No," he had replied. "The thing with these pills is that you can't tell if you're getting anything out of them or not unless you cut them out every once in a while. It takes will power to cut something out when the reason you've got the habit is that this something does something for you. But it takes a lot more will power to cut something out when the reason you've got the habit is just that you've got the habit. You follow me?"

"No," she had said.

"Look," he said, "the worst habits are the ones there's no excuse for. Right?"

"Right."

"So there you have it. If I have no excuse for taking the pills, it's a lousy habit. So I give it up every once in a while just to see if I can do it."

He was laughing, not with her but at her; at the same time, not with himself but at himself.

Now, lying there on the couch after supper while she did the dishes, he called in, "That way you never get forgotten."

"What?" she called. "What way?"

"Having a brother Willard who calls you every night."

"Sometimes he skips a night."

"How old is he?"

"Willard? Twenty-three. He's ten years younger than Mike."

"What does he do for kicks?"

"I don't know."

"Dirty pictures?"

"I never asked him," Emmy said.

"King Farouk collected dirty pictures," Gammon said.

"What's that got to do with Willard?"

"I was just asking."

"Why do you always keep prying?" Emmy said. "Does it say that's what you have to do? Does it say it on your press card?"

"No, but on my cutter pass it does," Gammon said. "Seems to me Willard pries more than I do."

"That's the way it seems to you."

"He calls every night. That's more than I do."

"You call every once in a while," she said.

"Not as much as Willard. How loyal. How faithful. How touching. How utterly decent."

"It's the way you say," Emmy said. "He doesn't want me to be forgotten."

"Do you whine and cry?" Gammon said.

"What?"

"Do you whine and cry? When you're forgotten?"

She looked at him. "What does that mean?"

"Dogs do," he said.

"They do?"

"Yes. Poetry. See, I do remember poetry. You're right. University of Chicago. You've got me tagged. Edwin Arlington Robinson. Only quote I know." He sighed some cigarette smoke toward the ceiling. "Ever hear of him?"

"Yes," Emmy said.

"Which is why I love you so desperately," Ben Gammon said, looking at the ceiling. "Think about it for a minute. How many people have heard of Edwin Arlington Robinson?"

"I have, and it's not much of a reason to love somebody desperately," Emmy said. "Go ahead. Tell me the lines."

"Lots of lines," he said. "Lots of lines, and I know them by heart. You want to hear them?"

"I said to."

"Okay. It goes:

> *A dog, when he's forgotten, whines and cries,*
> *Or looks and lets you know. Sometimes a woman*
> *Will only smile and ask you to keep warm*
> *When the wind blows. You do not see her face*

When you are gone, or guess what's in her mind
Or covered in her feelings, which are real
Beyond their reputation. It's a pity,
And a great shame, and a malevolent
Extravagance, that you should find that out
So often only when calamity
Comes down upon you like a broken house
To bring the news."

He broke off and was silent, and Emmy, standing in the doorway of the kitchen, said, "It's something, isn't it? It's really something. I never heard that before, Ben."

"Nor liable to hear it again, from me," he said.

"Ah, why not?" she said. "Why do you go and say something like that right away afterwards? You must think something about it, or you wouldn't have remembered it."

"It's the only piece of poetry I know," he said. "You want me to spend my life walking around quoting it? 'Malevolent extravagance.' That's nice, though, isn't it?"

"Tell it to me again," Emmy said.

"No," he said. "We'll start with meat loaf and make it a straight household evening all the way through. You can vacuum and I'll get the fights on the television." He yawned. "You'll wind up with twelve more reasons to marry the flyboy. Do you know how to work that television? How do we get the fights?"

"Must we?" Emmy said.

"It used to be a gag a few years ago," Gammon said. " 'We used to watch the fights at the neighbors' next door . . . then they got a television set.' Get it, doll baby love?"

"Anyway," Emmy said, "the fights don't go on till ten."

"What time is it now?"

She leaned back into the kitchen to look at the wall clock. "Not even ten of nine."

"Well," Gammon said. "An hour and ten minutes to kill. See now. Any ideas?"

"You could quote Edwin Arlington Robinson."

"For an hour and ten minutes?"

"Put your mind to it," Emmy said.

"I was putting my mind to something along somewhat different lines," Ben Gammon said. "But you're the right sort of girl."

"I am? What makes you say that?"

"You know what time the fights go on."

"Is ten o'clock right?"

"Ten o'clock's right."

"And what did you want to do till then?"

"Well, now," Gammon said. "If you would care to step closer over here for a mo, we could . . ."

"The phone," Emmy said, and went past him to answer the ringing.

"That will be the flyboy's brother Willard," Ben Gammon said, from the couch. "He spotted me on radar. Affirmative? Negative. Roger, willco, and out."

Emmy said into the telephone, "Hello? Oh. Hello, Willard."

"You have won the prize, sir," Gammon said to himself aloud. "A genuine sweetheart doll. She walks. She talks. She laughs, she cries, she revolves three hundred and six-ty degrees up-on a pedestal, sing-ing 'I Love You Truly.' Who's next, ladies and gentlemen, to try to win one of these . . ."

30

"A pencil?" Emmy said into the phone. "Wait a minute, Willard." She waved at Gammon and made a writing motion in the air. Gammon opened his palms in a gesture that asked her what newspaperman ever carried a pencil.

"Can't you tell it to me, I mean just tell it to me over the phone, Willard?" Emmy said. Then she shook her head, in concert with his answer. "No, you want me to write it down. You sound funny, Willard." She looked "stars above" at Ben Gammon. "Wait a minute." She set down the phone and went to the table in the foyer and found a pencil and some paper there and returned to the telephone. "All right, Willard. Read me the message and I'll write it down."

She wrote as he talked, and when he was through she said in a low voice, "Thank you," and slowly set the receiver back down in place. For a moment she stood there, not looking at anything.

Gammon said from the couch, "What was it?"

She did not say anything.

Gammon got up from the couch and went over to her and read the message over her shoulder. She had taken it down in a clear script, and the abbreviations she had used were instantly understandable, so there was no question about what it said:

FROM MIAMI AIR TRAF CONT FLIGHT 27 M OVRD BUT
THINK SEE RADAR—NO REPORT

The dramatist in Willard Trace had persuaded him to give her the message in this form.

Gammon said to her now, "Trace's plane?"

She nodded. "But he said it was more than twenty-seven minutes by now. I mean, it was twenty-seven minutes when *he* heard about it."

"Do you know what kind of planes they fly?"

She shook her head. "It takes off from Miami at seven-thirty. Due in here at a quarter to twelve."

"Nonstop," Gammon said, and she nodded again. "It would have to be four engines, then," he said. He put his hand on her shoulder, and her own hand came up to rest upon his own.

It was a moment of communion and comfort between them. There was no mistaking it.

With his free hand, Gammon took the telephone receiver off the hook, set it down so he could dial, then picked it up again and held it to his ear and, when the switchboard girl answered at the other end, said, "Give me the night desk. Fast."

AT 8:57 P.M., Washington was sending on the news-wire network of the Global Press Association, one of the largest of the wire services. Ben Gammon was only one of hundreds of reporters, correspondents, space-rate contacts, tip sources, and string men, all of whom supplied GPA with its news, but he was one of the best. A good reporter he was, and reliable when drunk, and this could be said of only a handful.

On the leased wire that served nearly a thousand news-papers and radio and television stations in the United States, the teletypes simultaneously told the news at their 60-word-a-minute pace:

NOT FEEL, THE SENATOR SAID, THAT THE COMMITTEE COULD OPERATE TO WHAT HE CALLED "FULL PURPOSE AND ADVANTAGE" UNLESS IT WAS GIVEN COMPLETE ACCESS TO ALL OF THE REQUESTED DATA.

BUT WHITE HOUSE SOURCES SAID A PRESIDENTIAL DIRECTIVE MADE IT IMPOSSIBLE FOR SUCH RECORDS TO BE TURNED OVER TO CONGRESSIONAL PROBERS.

MEANWHILE, TWO OF THE EIGHT WITNESSES SCHEDULED TO APPEAR NOTIFIED COMMITTEE AIDES THAT THEY WERE GGG

WHO BREAKS PLS?

NW BREAKING

BULLETIN

NEW YORK—COASTAL AIRLINES REPORTED TONIGHT THAT ONE OF ITS PLANES HAD FAILED TO MAKE SCHEDULED RADIO CONTACTS EN ROUTE NONSTOP FROM MIAMI TO NEW YORK.

THE FOUR-ENGINE CRAFT LEFT MIAMI AT 7:30 P.M. MIAMI TIME.

A PRELIMINARY REPORT INDICATED THE PLANE, FLYING ONE OF THE MAIN AIR ROUTES IN THE U. S., STILL COULD BE SEEN BY RADAR STATIONS ON THE GROUND.

IT WAS NOT IMMEDIATELY KNOWN HOW MANY PERSONS WERE ABOARD.

ALL EFFORTS SO FAR TO CONTACT THE PLANE BY RADIO HAVE FAILED.

859P/OPC   WASHN GO AHEAD

TO APPEAR NOTIFIED COMMITTEE AIDES THAT THEY WERE BEING ADVISED NOT TO TESTIFY UNTIL THE

CONTROVERSY OVER EXECUTIVE RECORDS HAD BEEN
SETTLED. ONE OF THE TWO WITNESSES, MALCOLM
BRIORDY OF DORCHESTER, MASS., TOLD NEWSMEN HE
HAD "BETTER THINGS TO DO THAN HANG AROUND
OUTSIDE

In the New York headquarters of the Global Press Association, the night editor and the rewrite man who had taken the bulletin from Gammon grinned at each other. It looked as if they had beat the other wire services hollow on this one.

MARSHALL KENT, Vice-President of Coastal Airlines in charge of Operations, was visiting tonight at the home of Felix Allerdyce, of Allerdyce & Watt, Advertising. The A & W agency had been after the Coastal account for four years, and tonight was as close to landing it as an ad agency could come without actually having signed contracts in hand. As a layman might view it, this was not particularly close. But Mr. Allerdyce, a handsome, hard-faced man in his fifties, was not a layman and had never been so accused.

Mr. Allerdyce was in trouble, at least at one point of the compass, because he was not a particularly nice man. This gave him something of a vantage point, at least in dealing with other men; but this vantage was canceled in this one case because Marshall Kent, of Coastal Airlines, was, if that was possible, even less of a nice man than Allerdyce. At best they were even going in, and it was, to Allerdyce, somewhat bewildering.

In his youth, Allerdyce had earned money being a male

model, posing with a towel around his neck and a tennis racket and smiling at the girl in the bathing suit or the girl in the new convertible, or at the three other guys, all wielding mashies and standing, one foot on clubhouse bench, in their underwear.

Perhaps the exigencies of this kind of work had exercised their influence on Allerdyce. It was essential, back in those days, to change clothes fast; and this factor may indeed have contributed to Allerdyce's present philosophy, which was that his success in advertising traced back essentially to the postulate that speed was the most essential part of the entire business. It was in its way an unusual method of looking at things, but for Felix Allerdyce it had paid off. If a client wanted a survey taken, Allerdyce could get him the results inside of five days, even if it took half his office staff four straight days of overtime to phony up the figures.

One result of this philosophy, aside from its successes (and legion they were), was the contempt it bred in Allerdyce for his life's work. It was only occasionally that he found himself truly enjoying his profession.

Tonight, though, was one of those times.

He had a mock-up of a series of ads to show to Kent, a new sales campaign for Coastal Airlines, and the ads were tied together with a new slogan. Allerdyce knew clients' weaknesses for slogans, but this one for Coastal was a different matter. It was more than a slogan. It was a small, shining, creative gem. Felix Allerdyce had, in point of actual fact, thought this one up himself.

"It came to me," he said to Kent now, "in a blinding flash." They were having coffee in the library of Allerdyce's home in Riverdale, New York. "You know what I mean. The way a headache comes on." Allerdyce laughed boyishly.

"Mine come on slowly," Kent said. He was a roundish, blunt, unsentimental type, highly excitable and apt to say the first thing that came into his head. "What I got actually is a neuralgia. It can be in the ear, or the jaw, or over the eye, or I can get a sensation of coldness in the entire area."

"While I was working on this presentation for you," Allerdyce said smoothly, maneuvering the conversation back to advertising without making it seem as if he were cutting the other man short or, in fact, even altering the subject matter at all, "I had something of the same thing. The doctor told me, 'It's the pressure of your job.' He said, 'The minute . . .'"

"That's not what the doctor told me," Kent said.

"No?" Allerdyce said.

"No," Kent said. "In diabetics, the sugar in sugar is harmful because the body isn't producing enough insulin, which counteracts sugar. In the opposite from diabetes, which is what I got, the carbohydrates in sugar are harmful because they stimulate further production of insulin, which the body is already producing too much of. Do you see this?"

"Of course," Allerdyce said.

"Hyperinsulinism," Kent said, "is what I got."

"Ah," Allerdyce said. "But when you stop *thinking* about it . . ."

Marshall Kent said, "Who stops thinking about it?"

"My doctor," Allerdyce said smoothly, "told me, 'It's the pressure of your job.' That's what he said to me. 'The minute whatever you're working on at the moment crystal-

36

lizes, that kind of pain goes away.' That's what the doctor told me. And by George he was right. Wait till you see this . . ."

"Mine doesn't go away," Kent said.

"Think up a slogan like this one and it would," Allerdyce said, and laughed. "A blinding flash. That's what it was."

"Only on the right side of my face," Kent said.

"Mine was the same," Allerdyce said. "But the minute the idea came to me, it . . . well, let me show you. Something like this can cure a man's ills."

He hoped devoutly that he was not spreading it on too thick; with a man like Kent you could never tell. The advertising business was a strange one. Allerdyce's favorite idea had been prompted once by an advertisement in a magazine for the Pullman Company, showing a man getting off a train fresh and relaxed after a night's journey, and the slogan was, "The miles never show." It struck Allerdyce immediately that the word "miles" also was a man's first name. He got up a presentation for a television show, to be sponsored by Pullman, which would feature an actor with the name of Miles Never. This then would become The Miles Never Show. But nothing came of it.

"Hyperinsulinism," Kent said now. "I had three teeth pulled before I found out it wasn't the teeth at all."

Another approach suggested itself to Allerdyce. "You know," he said, "there's one hell of a pill on the market now. Might fix you up." He smiled. "One of our clients."

"I've tried them all," Kent said.

"This one's brand-new," Allerdyce said. He looked at his watch. "Five of nine. We've got a twenty-second commercial spot on Channel 6, coming up at nine o'clock. Let's turn it on and you can see it for yourself. See one

37

of our ads in action, too." (The trouble with it was, for Allerdyce, that idea he'd had was so good he could never turn on television without hearing in his mind's ear a burst of fanfare and an announcer proclaiming, "The Miles Never Show . . . ! brought to you by the Pullman Company." It was, to him, like that horrible "Punch, Brothers, Punch" jingle celebrated by Mark Twain.)

But business was business.

"I've seen your ads," Kent said now.

To Allerdyce, as he turned on the television set and adjusted it, the Coastal contract, what with one thing and another, seemed somehow to have receded somewhat in the last minute or two. He wished something would happen to provide a distraction so that the conversation could at this juncture be switched entirely.

His wish was rewarded. The door to the library opened and Jenner, the butler, stood there with a portable telephone in his hand.

"Excuse me, sir," Jenner said. "Telephone for Mr. Kent. Shall I plug it in here?"

"Thank you, Jenner," Allerdyce said, and smiled. "Probably some other ad man, Marshall."

"I hope he's got pills too," Marshall Kent said. "I'll try them all." He picked up the phone and said, "Yes?"

The voice of Willard Trace at the other end said, "Mr. Kent, this is the Operations Office at LaGuardia."

"Whose Operations Office?" Kent asked.

"Yours," Trace said. "I called your home, sir, and they told me . . ."

"Well, what is it?"

"Our flight number 214, sir," Trace said. "It's overdue reporting; must be near an hour now."

"What do you mean, overdue?"

"He hasn't reported."

"To who?"

"Whoever he's supposed to report to. Air Traffic Control."

"Is he down?"

"No, sir."

"What's your name again?"

"Trace."

"Don't keep any bad news from me, Trace. I can take it."

"No, sir. Yes, sir."

"How do you know he's not down?"

"They have a radar contact on him."

"Well, what does he say?"

"He says he can't contact him."

"Who says who can't contact who?"

"The radar."

"Well, what does the *plane* say, for Christ's sake?"

"He doesn't say anything, sir," Trace said. "That's what I'm trying to tell you. They can't make contact. They just can't raise him by radio."

"Well, that makes no sense at all," Kent said. "Where is he from and where's he going?"

"Miami to New York. Nonstop."

"That's the only kind we fly."

"Yes, sir."

"Well, what's the matter with that pilot?" Kent said. "What is he, asleep?"

"It's my brother, sir," Trace said.

"Your brother sleeps the same as the rest of us, doesn't he? What's *his* name?"

"The same as mine, sir," Trace said. "Because he's my brother."

"What's his *name?*"

"Mike Trace."

"Who are you?"

"Willard Trace."

"Between the two of you you're doing fine tonight, aren't you?" Kent uttered a terrible laugh. "Fine and dandy, hey?"

"I don't know, sir."

"Well, a man doesn't fly without talking to somebody about it. It's against the rules. Don't you know that?"

"Yes, sir."

"It's not done, that's all. If he's crashed it's one thing. But if he's just cruising through the skies up there, it's something else."

"They think his radios are out," Willard Trace said.

"Well, send him a message to fix them," Kent said. "That's what flight crews are for."

"Yes, sir," Trace said, "but . . ."

"And if he can't fix them, tell him to land someplace. Where is he now?"

"How can we tell him anything," Willard Trace said plaintively, "if he can't . . ."

"I said where is he now?"

"Almost an hour-and-a-half out of Miami."

"But you said he was an hour overdue reporting."

"Yes, sir."

"Then if he's in trouble it must have happened only a half hour after take-off."

"Even before that," Trace said.

"That's right," Kent said. "Likely so. It must have happened *before* he was due to report."

"Yes, sir."

"You're a smart fellow, Trace."

"Thank you, sir."

"You should be flying that plane and your brother should be sitting on his ass where you are."

"Yes, sir," Willard Trace said.

"Because if it happened that early, then he would have turned around and gone back. Wouldn't he?"

"I don't know."

"What do you mean, you don't know? He's your brother, isn't he?"

"Yes, sir."

"Well, what kind of a . . . wait a minute. Did you say Flight 214?"

"Yes, sir."

"Isn't that the one that's half passenger, half cargo?"

"Yes, sir," Trace said. "The Everyinch."

"The what?"

"The Everyinch. That's what they call it, sir."

"That's what who calls it?"

"The boys."

"The boys? What boys?"

"Some of the boys, sir."

"Some of the boys are going to get straightened out pretty good before this night's over," Kent said. "Do you know what's in that cargo, Trace?"

"A dog," Willard Trace said.

"I'm not talking about a dog," Kent said. "Know what else?"

"No, sir."

"Fish," Kent said.

Trace said hopelessly, "Fish?"

"Fish," Kent said. "Fish, fish, fish. First shipment. A new

exclusive contract. I wrote the contract myself. Went into effect today. Sixty New York restaurants and a Miami wholesaler. Florida sea food daily. Flown to New York by Coastal Airlines. Thousands of dollars. Long-term contract."

"Yes, sir," Trace said.

"So first crack out of the box, what do we do as the exclusive carrier?" Kent said. "Apparently, what we do is this. We're figuring on putting the fish back in the ocean the hard way. That's what it looks like to me."

"He's in *trouble*, sir," Trace said. "He's got *passengers*."

"He would," Kent said. "Do you have this number here?"

"Yes, sir."

"Call me as soon as you hear something."

"I will," Trace said.

"And you know the most important thing of all?"

"No, sir."

"Don't talk it around. You understand? I don't want the papers hearing about it."

"No, sir."

"If he's up there and on course then there's nothing seriously wrong," Kent said. "Nobody has to know this happened."

"All right, sir," Willard Trace said.

Kent put down the phone and turned to Allerdyce, who was watching the television screen.

"It's always something," Kent said. "My headache's worse."

"I'm deeply sorry to hear it," Felix Allerdyce said.

"I suppose I missed that commercial?"

"They didn't run it."

42

"I thought you said it was going to be on."

"They'll put it on half an hour from now," the advertising man said. "They subbed it out this time for a news bulletin."

"We're having trouble with a plane," Kent told him.

"That was the bulletin," Allerdyce said.

So the American public knew about it at nine o'clock. There was not much to the initial report on radio and television, and of what little there was, not all was wholly accurate.

But the public knew, and reacted.

In Minneapolis, a woman turned to her husband. "That's the plane *I* was on."

"How the hell do you know?" he said.

"We left Miami at seven-thirty at night," she said. "So did this plane."

"For holy hopper's sake, Agnes," her husband said. "That was two years ago and it was a different airline and the plane was flying to a different place."

"Lottie was with me."

"Oh, that makes it official," the husband said. "Wrap that one up. Lottie was with you. You haven't even talked to Lottie for six months now."

"Well, I'm going to call her on the phone right now this instant," the wife said. "All it was between us was a misunderstanding. We've just been out of touch. That's all."

"It was so peaceful around here," the husband said. "All of a sudden a plane crashes a thousand miles from noplace and I got to put up with Lottie again."

Or—in Shelbyville, Tennessee—a twenty-one-year-old girl who wanted to be an airline stewardess began to argue it all over again with her father.

"Hedley Markow is a good, conservative farm boy," her father said. "I say marry him and raise a family and live off the land the way your people always have."

"We've been all through this," the girl said miserably.

"What's wrong with Hedley Markow?"

"It's not a question of what's wrong with Hedley Markow. If I want to have a career as an airline stewardess before I settle down, I don't see what that has to do with Hedley Markow. I don't see what's so terrible about . . ."

"The danger, that's what's so terrible," the father said. "You're the only girl your ma and me have got. Your mother's feeling poorly these last two years and you know it. You've got a duty, that's what you've got."

"It pays well," the girl said.

"Hedley Markow makes a good living too. If you marry him, you can give some of his earnings to your mother and myself."

The girl said, "That wouldn't be right."

"Raise chickens yourself, on the farm," her father said. "The earnings from the chickens are what you can pass on to your mother."

"I don't want to raise chickens," the girl said. "I want to fly."

"It's dangerous."

"It isn't dangerous."

"Got eyes and ears, haven't you?" the father said. "Just saw it and heard it on the television, didn't you?"

"Flying's less dangerous than driving a car," the girl said.

"Not if you get a real careful driver like Hedley Markow," the father said.

Or—in Portland, Maine—a lawyer who had scheduled a trip to Washington three weeks hence began to reconsider his plans. Originally, he had planned to go by train. But now, he said to his wife, "Know something? Maybe I'll fly. Be a much shorter trip that way."

"But you just heard about that plane on the radio," his wife said.

"I know," he said, "and I know those airlines. Every time they have a crash, they take extra pains checking the planes beforehand. For the next month or so, there'll be no safer way to travel than to fly."

Or—not a specific individual effect, but a much more general one—at airport after airport throughout the country, beginning shortly after nine o'clock as passengers arrived after having heard the news bulletin on automobile radios: it was not a spectacular effect, but veteran airport personnel noticed it at once, and knew—even those of them who had not heard about it—that something had befallen a plane somewhere.

The coin-operated machines that wrote flight insurance for on-boarding passengers started getting a heavy play.

BEN GAMMON had mixed Emmy a stiff drink, and she was sitting apart from him on the sofa, her legs pulled up under her and her hand holding the glass white and tense.

"Think of it," he said. "Just think of it." She did not

answer, and he went on: "Faced with an emergency, what does the great reporter forget to do?"

"I didn't think the great reporter forgot anything."

"He forgot to make a drink for himself." He looked at her. "All right?"

"I don't care," she said.

"I'm sorry," he said. He stood up. "Can I take you someplace?"

"Where?"

"I don't know."

"His brother may call again."

"That's right," Gammon said.

"He said he would," Emmy said.

"That's right," Gammon said again. "Is your drink all right?"

"Yes."

"Well, drink it, then. It'll give you a better feeling."

She placed her lips dutifully to the rim of the glass.

He said, "Do you want me to go away?"

"If you want to."

"I don't want to."

"Your wire service may need you," she said.

"I'm off. I'm not working."

"You called them pretty fast before," she said. "You're always working."

"Yes, sure," he said. "Printer's ink instead of blood."

"By all means stay here," she said. "This seems to be the place where the news comes first."

"I'm sorry, Emmy," he said. "I didn't plan this."

"You plan everything else," she said. "Too bad for you."

"I said I was sorry."

"No more poetry?" Emmy said. "No Swinburne?"

"Look," he said, "you want me to get out of here?"

She studied her glass for a time. "No," she said at last. "It's nice to have company."

"Sure." He nodded. "I'm going to mix myself a drink."

"On your way back," she said, "turn off the television."

"Really? You want it off?"

"Yes."

"Now that the news is out, they may hear something faster than we do."

Emmy said nothing.

"There'll be other sources of information now," Gammon said. "The television might have something."

Still she said nothing.

"Better leave it on," he advised, and went into the kitchen to make himself a drink. While he was there, the phone rang, and he watched Emmy as she went to answer it.

He was back in the room with his drink by the time she was through.

"Willard?" he said.

She nodded.

"Any news?"

"No. They heard that a plane took off from Miami after Mike's plane and didn't report any weather that you'd have to . . . you know . . ."

"Keep radio silence for?"

"Yes, that's it." Something of a smile came to her face. "Willard's very upset. He said a man named Marshall Kent was very angry with him over the telephone."

"Who's Marshall Kent? A muck-a-muck with Coastal?"

"I guess so," Emmy said. "A vice-president or something."

"But they can still see the plane on radar?"

"He didn't say."

"Then they can," Gammon said. "If something had happened to change that, Willard would have told you." It occurred to him wryly that he was talking like an insurance agent. If the plane was no longer visible on radar screens, that meant it had crashed. But he could not, would not bring himself to use that terminology. What was it that insurance man had said to him, the phrase he had used as a substitute for the word "die"? Gammon could not remember it exactly. It had been something about "if you check out of the picture"—something like that.

Now he said, "How many people on the plane? Does Willard know?"

"He didn't say. I didn't ask him. Mike's on it. That much we know."

"Let's find out," Gammon said, and he went to the phone and dialed his office and learned that Global Press had not yet been able to contact the public relations man for the airline; that Miami was trying there; but no word yet on a passenger list.

"It's a crazy airline," the man on the desk told Gammon over the phone. "Their head offices are here but they actually do most of their flying over swamps someplace way the hell else."

An idea came to Gammon. He said to Emmy, "What was that? Marshall Kent?"

She nodded. "All right," Gammon said into the phone. "Get that airlines-railroad-steamship personnel thing you've got in the drawer there and see if they mention somebody named Kent—Marshall Kent—with Coastal."

"I've got it in front of me," the desk man at GPA

said. "Kent . . . Coastal Airlines . . . Kent . . . who would . . . wait—Here it is. Marshall Kent. Vice-President in charge of Operations."

"I'll call him for you," Gammon said. "Give me something to do."

Then he hung up the phone and called Kent's number, and the voice there, as it had for Willard Trace, gave him Felix Allerdyce's home phone. Gammon hung up and called the new number, told the butler who answered who he was, and shortly had Kent on the phone.

"Gammon of Global Press," Ben said. "Are you the Mr. Kent of Coastal Airlines?"

"What's it to you if I am?" Kent said.

"Not a hell of a lot," Gammon said. "But you've announced this plane business and we . . ."

"I," Kent broke in, "haven't announced anything, and when I find the guy who did, I'll break his . . ."

"Well," the newspaperman said, "tell me. Are they all nice fellas like you over at the hangar?"

"You'd better say what you want," Kent said. "And quick about it."

Gammon said, "Passenger list."

"Passenger list?"

"You sound like you don't believe it."

"Listen," Kent said, "what makes you think I have a passenger list? You think I carry them around with me? You think I've got one in my pocket?"

"After tonight you'll probably have room in your pocket for that airline's passenger lists," Gammon said smoothly. "No, we can't raise your P.R.O., and I thought perhaps you could tell me where I could get ahold of the list the quickest—here or Miami or where?"

"What makes you think you can get ahold of it at all?"

"Oho," Ben Gammon said.

"Oho," Marshall Kent said to him.

"Okay," Gammon said. "Can I get ahold of it at all?"

"No," Kent said.

"And what title do you hold with the airline?"

"Why?"

"So we can credit the source when our next bulletin says the airline refused to say who was on board this aircraft, or how many people."

"What do you mean, 'refused'?"

"That's our word for it," Gammon said. "It's press-association English, meaning to refuse."

"You newspapermen think you're entitled to anything, don't you? Anything and everything."

"The difference between anything and everything," Ben Gammon said, "is the core of a free press."

"You're smarter than I am," Kent said to him. "I don't understand that at all."

"I was oversimplifying," Gammon said.

"I don't understand that either."

"That makes it tough all around."

"And none of this," Kent said, "gets you any closer to a passenger list. Now, does it?"

"Why, no," Gammon said. "It doesn't. So we'll play it that way. Your way. We'll say Mr. Marshall Kent refused to allow us to get the passenger list and then refused to say what position he held with the airline. Notice the use of the word 'held' in the past tense, Mr. Kent. There. That way all your little secrets are intact."

"I get it," Kent said.

"And good luck on your next job," Gammon said.

"I don't know you, but I think you're a son-of-a-bitch," Kent said into the phone.

"People who know me say the same," Gammon said. "Look, what about the list?"

There was a pause. Then Kent said, "Miami would be the place. Have your man there or your bureau or whatever it is call our airport number."

"Thank you," Gammon said. "Will your man down there need any okay to release it?"

"Give me five minutes to get them on the phone."

"You might tell them to give us all the information they have, while you're at it."

"The camel moves into the tent pretty fast, doesn't he? I thought all you wanted was a passenger list."

Gammon said gently, "You want the news to be accurate, don't you? You don't want us going and crossing you up. You don't want us picking up dribs and drabs here and there."

"I don't care what you do," Kent said.

"You've been kind," Gammon said. "I'll have Miami ring your boy in five minutes."

At 9:28 P.M., GPA had the passenger list on its wires, and within two more minutes the other major wire services, caught up by now, had it too.

This was the list:

TRACE, Michael R., 33, flight captain, Roslyn Heights, N. Y.

BELDING, Kenneth, 37, first officer, Donora, Pa.

GOLDSTONE, Marvin, 42, flight engineer, Boston, Mass.

LOFTUS, Barbara Ruth, 20, stewardess, Anaheim, Calif.
WEBBER, Mrs. Albie, Tenafly, N. J.
WEBBER, Jane, 5, Tenafly, N. J.
SHERMAN, Mrs. K. L., New York City, N. Y.
DIAZ, Rafael, San Juan, Puerto Rico
DIAZ, Mrs. R., San Juan, Puerto Rico
DIAZ, Roberto, 7, San Juan, Puerto Rico
DIAZ, Luis, 11, San Juan, Puerto Rico
DIAZ, infant child, San Juan, Puerto Rico
BLACK, John
LAURIE, James, Brooklyn, N. Y.
LAURIE, Mrs. James, Brooklyn, N. Y.
JONAS, Herman, Miami, Fla.

There was something about the list that made it stand apart from lists so much like it that the wire services handled every time there was a plane disaster. Something —it was easy to define, yet it defied simple analysis. One answer could have been the number of children, in ratio to the total number of passengers. Another could have been the grim absurdity of a giant four-engine plane taking off from Miami nonstop for New York with a full crew of four, a nearly-filled passenger cabin, a jammed freight load, yet only, in actuality, twelve passengers.

Coastal Airlines in Miami explained the physical make-up of the Everyinch—only twenty seats, the rest cargo. That added to the unusual nature of the list too.

But most of all, it was the time element.

In all other cases, the names of the passengers on the planes became known only after the planes crashed.

But as far as anyone knew at this particular moment, Coastal 214 was still in the sky.

And one more factor—another part of the time element. The fact that a passenger list was available ahead of the actual disaster made it a born newspaper story. The fact that the passenger list was as short as it was made it feasible to read the names over radio and television.

And by sheer coincidence, the first bulletin had reached radio and TV newsrooms just before the 9:00 (Eastern Time) break; the second, just before 9:30.

So for the second time Felix Allerdyce, the ad man, saw his commercial spot for the neuralgia pill wiped out.

The other wire services had the story by now, but Global Press still had more information. GPA's bulletin lead, hitting TV and radio in time for the 9:30 program break, said:

A FOUR-ENGINE COASTAL AIRLINES PLANE WITH FOUR CHILDREN AND TWELVE OTHERS ON BOARD IS NOW WELL OVER AN HOUR OVERDUE FOR A SCHEDULED RADIO CONTACT IN THE EARLY PART OF ITS NONSTOP FLIGHT FROM MIAMI TO NEW YORK. BUT THE AIRLINE SAYS THE PLANE IS NOT (REPEAT N O T) PRESUMED TO BE LOST.

THIS HOPE APPARENTLY IS BASED ON EARLIER REPORTS THAT EVEN AFTER ATTEMPTS AT RADIO CONTACT HAD FAILED ENTIRELY, THE HUGE CRAFT STILL WAS VISIBLE TO GROUND OBSERVERS VIA RADAR.

AT THE SAME TIME, A THEORY THAT THE FLIGHT, KNOWN AS COASTAL FLIGHT 214, MIGHT BE KEEPING RADIO SILENCE DUE TO STORM CONDITIONS —AN UNLIKELY BUT STILL POSSIBLE EXPLANATION—WAS DISCARDED WHEN ANOTHER PLANE, LEAVING MIAMI FOR NEW YORK MINUTES AFTER THE COASTAL FLIGHT, REPORTED NO SUCH TURBULENCE.

WHILE RAIN AND CLOUDED SKIES PREVAIL ALONG THE ENTIRE EASTERN SEABOARD, WEATHER CONDI-

TIONS WERE NOT REPORTED AS RESEMBLING THOSE WHICH MIGHT DICTATE SUCH UNUSUAL CONDITIONS OF RADIO SILENCE.

DESPITE THE RAINS THAT ARE LASHING THE COAST IN ADVANCE OF THE SEASON'S FIRST HURRICANE, THE COASTAL PLANE'S SCHEDULED FLIGHT ALTITUDE WOULD HAVE TAKEN THE CRAFT ABOVE THE CLOUDS IN THE AREA OFF THE NORTHERN FLORIDA COAST WHERE HIS RADIO REPORT TO THE CIVIL AERONAUTICS AUTHORITY'S AIR TRAFFIC CONTROL WAS TO BE MADE.

AN UNUSUAL NOTE WAS ADDED BY THE FACT THAT MOST OF THE PLANE'S CABIN SPACE IS RESERVED FOR CARGO, SAID TO RANGE FROM JEWELRY TO BARKING DOGS.

A FAMILY OF FIVE—MR. AND MRS. RAFAEL DIAZ AND THEIR THREE CHILDREN, ALL OF PUERTO RICO—WERE LISTED AS BEING ABOARD THE PLANE.

ANOTHER CHILD WAS FIVE-YEAR-OLD JANE WEBBER OF TENAFLY, NEW JERSEY, TRAVELING WITH HER MOTHER, MRS. ALBIE WEBBER. ATTEMPTS WERE BEING MADE TO LEARN IF THEY WERE THE WIFE AND CHILD OF ALBIE WEBBER, WELTERWEIGHT BOXING CONTENDER SCHEDULED TO OPPOSE WOLF HAGAN AT ST. NICHOLAS ARENA TONIGHT IN A NATIONALLY TELEVISED TEN-ROUNDER.

THE PLANE WAS PILOTED BY MICHAEL R. TRACE, 33 YEARS OLD.

In the Global Press newsroom in New York, Harry Timmons, the lead night rewrite man, was pounding it out. It was surprising how much story could be made to flow from such terse and sparse data. The practice of the airlines in listing the ages of all children under twelve, for fare purposes at the ticket counters, told a tale all its own. The briefest description of the cargo make-up of the Everyinch, from a Coastal Airlines man in Miami who was trying, as much as anything else, to justify the brevity of the passenger list, enabled Timmons to get off the line "from jewelry to barking dogs," which was a line he liked. He did not know about the fish, or he would have included them too.

Timmons looked up from his typewriter and saw that Max Wild, the general manager of GPA, had come into the newsroom. Wild had been working late in his office and had heard the clanging of the bulletin bells on the teletype machine installed near his desk.

The general manager was a small, spidery man who wore thick horn-rimmed eyeglasses and walked like a careful cat. Timmons saw that he had a copy of the bulletin matter in his hand.

"I heard we were ahead," Wild said. It was the first thing he said.

"Beat the others solid," Timmons said.

"Where'd we get it?"

"Ben Gammon."

"Where'd he get it?"

"Nobody's got around to asking him."

"You mean he just phoned it in unverified?"

Timmons shrugged. "It came from Gammon."

"Is he drunk?"

"No more than usual."

"Is he?"

"How the hell do I know?" Timmons said. "It's his day off."

"Oh, great," Max Wild said.

"Listen," Timmons said, "it checks out. As much as we know, anyway. The passenger list and all. The other services are carrying the same thing by now."

"I still don't like it," the general manager said. "Damn it, we ought to lay down some kind of standard operating procedure on things like this."

"Come off it, Max," Timmons said. "You're not making a speech at the Waldorf. Let me tell you about one time at GPA in Chicago, years ago—so many years ago that at night Chicago was responsible for the whole United States from West Virginia to the Rockies, because there wasn't another bureau operating at night. And a phone call came collect from some crazy place in Texas, and the guy on the desk in the Chicago bureau accepted the charges, even though he didn't know who was calling and we didn't have any money in those days to pay for phone calls like that, and it turned out it was a guy tipping us off to an explosion in a school, and we went ahead and put it on the wire, and . . ."

". . . and the man on the desk in Chicago that night was Max Wild," Max Wild said. "All right. Okay. I know."

"Three cheers for the Jones Junior High," Harry Timmons said. "Gammon's a good newspaperman."

"I know it," the general manager said. "Well. Are we up to date? What are we doing?"

"Sports is checking the boxer to see if it's the same one," Timmons said. "I've got a phone number for where Gammon is, and he's got some kind of a pipeline to the airline up here, but by now Miami's feeding us stuff and they're getting in touch with the CAA down there."

Wild pursed his lips. "There's a story in here."

Harry Timmons uttered a short laugh. "There're a hundred stories in there. It's going to be a honey."

"You think he's still flying?"

"Hell, no."

"Then he's down."

"Yup."

"What about that business about seeing him on radar?"

Timmons shrugged. "Don't forget, we've got this way ahead of the usual time for one of these stories. Confusion —sure. That radar thing was more than an hour ago— maybe even longer than that. And besides, if you can't talk to a guy and he can't talk to you, how do you even know it's him? This always happens. First the report is the plane's overdue, with all the usual gismo that goes with it—maybe keeping radio silence because of weather and so forth; then it's overdue and presumed lost, but not till hours after the guy actually goes down. The difference here is we caught 'em with their press agents at half mast. Gammon ought to get the Pulitzer Prize just for that."

"You're right," Wild said. "He's got to be down."

"In the water, best as I can make it," Timmons said.

"But I don't know," Wild said, a little doubtfully. "I don't recall seeing the bit about having the plane on radar as part of the standard excuses. That's something new."

"New, because they've only recently been equipping more Air Traffic Control stations with radar," Timmons said pedantically. "After that crash over the Grand Canyon."

"But," Wild said, "it's like you said. How do they know it's him, and how long ago was the radar report?" He blinked. "Sixteen people on the plane. If he is down, it's not a real big one."

"Except for maybe that fighter having his wife and kid on it," Timmons said. "And another thing. Suppose he goes down and has to ditch. He's flying a commercial route over water. So he's got life jackets—I think those planes have rafts too. We're in on it from the start. Dramatic sea rescue."

"Why didn't you get that in the story?"

"It's only a possibility."

"Get it in anyway. As a possibility."

"Just about to do that," Timmons said blandly.

Max Wild tapped the copy in his hand. "Getting back to what I said about there being a story in here. You passed right over it."

"What?" Timmons said, craning his neck to see. "Where?"

"About this second plane that took off for New York right after the first one."

"What about it?"

"That Grand Canyon you were talking about," Wild said. "Remember?"

Timmons said slowly, "Oh, oh, oh. Ohh, yes." He turned and shouted over to the desk man, "Gene, get Miami on the phone. We can get our signals straight on the story, and while you've got him ask him to check that second plane that took off after the first one."

He turned back to his typewriter and began to work again. Max Wild looked at him for a moment, watching him work, then turned and walked over to one of the sample teletype machines that were reproducing the GPA news report as it went out over the wires.

He did not notice the passage of time—but it could not have been long before he became aware that Harry Timmons was standing beside him.

"That was a good idea of yours," Timmons said.

"About a mid-air collision?"

The rewrite man nodded. "Miami checked and said that second plane is one of those special flights. Chartered to fly army servicemen and their families. You know."

"How many people aboard?"

"Miami isn't sure. They have a preliminary figure, but they're checking."

"What was the preliminary figure?"

"Ninety-one," Timmons said.

THERE OUGHT to be a song with that title," Arnold Keller said to himself. " 'My Girl Friend's Widowed Mother.' " He was on his way, in his father's car, to visit the mother of Barbara Ruth Loftus, stewardess tonight on Coastal 214. Coastal 214 was a long ways off—by now, had it been on uneventful course, it would be somewhere off the Carolina coast, and here was Arnold Keller, four miles from Anaheim, California, jammed up in suburban Los Angeles traffic.

But Barbara's mother had asked him out for the evening, and it was wise to obey Barbara's mother. It made Arnold Keller feel more secure about Barbara: at least her mother liked him. With Barbara herself, Keller could never tell. She was beautiful and fond, but there was an elusiveness about her that confounded her swain. He had the feeling always that she had a man in every port, and she showed no inclination to come down out of the sky.

Arnold Keller was jealous, by turn of nature, and the situation preyed upon him. The way to work it was to work on Barbara's mother; thus gladly he had accepted the old lady's invitation to come out tonight (old lady—she was barely fifty, but Keller himself was barely twenty).

It would be a terrifying evening; this Keller knew beforehand. Barbara's mother would want to play Russian Bank, the only card game she knew, and Arnold hated Russian Bank. On top of that, she insisted on serving him supper, and her suppers were dietary horrors, devoid of sugar, caffeine, carbohydrates, and all dairy products. Supper at Mrs. Loftus' seemed at times to Keller to consist of one long drink of V-8 juice. He doubted not that it was healthy, but he had his youth to consider.

His youth—and Barbara. He considered Barbara now, while the radio in his car played softish music, and actually he did not feel that he knew too much about her, even though they had gone to UCLA together. He loved her; of this he was certain. Part of the jealousy was bound up in this. He could even take her mother as part of the marriage ceremony, and such the mother seemed destined to be.

The mother was a nut, no doubt about it. She was always having visions and images and dreams, besides the diets and the Russian Bank. But she seemed to like Arnold Keller. At times he wondered whether she fretted over Barbara as much as he did. Right now—at this moment— he did not even know where Barbara was. He knew she was flying for Coastal and would be going into New York, but he did not know the actual details until, at 6:30 Pacific Time, the radio cut in with the Global Press data on the Everyinch, together with the passenger list, and then Arnold Keller knew.

The news bulletin had scarcely gone off the air when he drove up in front of Mrs. Loftus' house. He entered the house not knowing what to say; what was worse, neither the radio nor the television was turned on, so the mother did not know, and he would have to tell her.

So Arnold Keller thought, but he was surprised.

"Arnold, oh, Arnold," Barbara's mother said to him at the door. "The most terrible thing has happened."

He nodded.

"I was lying there on the couch," she said. "I must have fallen asleep for a minute. Suddenly I saw it."

"Saw it?"

"Barbara's plane." She put a hand to her heart. "Falling. Plunging. Straight down into the sea."

part two: THE GROUNDLINGS

Herb Lenz, the boxing writer for the Global Press Association, got the message from his Western Union telegraph operator at ringside at St. Nicholas Arena in New York, where Lenz was sitting dismally watching the next-to-last preliminary bout on the evening's boxing card.

Lenz stared at the message, written in the telegrapher's

ornate script on a piece of Western Union press-copy paper. Then he said, "Always something," and took the message and eased himself out of the front row and down the ramp of the aisle to the dressing room of Albie Webber, the fighter.

The evidence was there. The other wire services, and with them the newspapers themselves, had caught up on the story. Lenz saw four other local boxing writers grouped outside the dressing room. Their way was blocked by the giant presence of an old-time heavyweight fighter, gone punchy early and lastingly in his career, Hatsky Gideon. Hatsky was a caricature of a caricature. He was everything the dumb, sense-deadened heavyweight fighter was expected to be, and some besides. The local boxing club paid him fifty-seven dollars a week, partly out of the goodness of its heart and partly because there were odd jobs like this that had to be done by someone, jobs that in fact suffered when pursued either with imagination or common sense. Hatsky, patently and fortunately, had neither. He had been told to insulate the fighter within from the approach of anyone—*anyone*—and this he was doing.

"Hatsky," one of the sports writers was saying, "his wife and kid have crashed on a———plane. Don't that mean nothing to you?"

"You don't tell me what to do," Hatsky said to him.

"What do you mean, I don't tell you what to do? What's that got to do with anything?"

"The promoter tells me what to do," Hatsky said.

"The promoter don't *know* it yet," the writer said.

"I know what you said about me when I lost that fight to Baer," Hatsky said to him. He nodded heavily. "I know.

You think I'm dumb? You think I can't read what's in the papers? I know. You know that? I know!"

Another writer said, "Hatsky, look. That don't make any difference to what we're saying now."

"I got my orders," Hatsky said.

"Look," a third boxing writer said, "this man has just lost his wife and daughter on an airplane. Do you understand what I'm trying to tell you?"

"Yuh, I understand," Hatsky said. His voice was set perpetually in an uneducated growl. "What're you trying to do? Upset him?"

Herb Lenz looked at the other writers. "Do we know that it *is* his wife and kid? For sure?"

"Damn right we know it," one of the writers said.

"Has anybody talked to him?"

"How can you talk to him? Monstro here won't let you in."

"Then how do you know?"

"Look," the other writer said. "It all checks out. Albie's from Tenafly. We know he's got a wife and a kid about the age of the one on the passenger list."

"And the kid's name is Jane," one of the other writers said. "So it checks."

"And they were in Miami seeing some of her people," one of the others said.

"And how many Albie Webbers of any kind are there?" another said.

"Especially from Tenafly?" Still another.

"Well," Lenz said, "I guess that's it."

"Sure it's it," one of the writers said. "But try to sell the Whale here something like that."

"You want to upset him," Hatsky Gideon said. "All of

you." He turned accusingly upon one of the older writers. "Like the time you come and talked to me just before I was going to fight Baer."

"He lives to be a hundred, he'll never get that Baer fight out of his head," the writer said.

One of the others said, "Hatsky, make sense, will you please? You want to do us a favor?"

"I got my orders, that's the way I make sense," Hatsky said. "What do you want to do? Rush me? Come on. I'll take y' on, all of y's." He flattened his back against the door of the dressing room.

Herb Lenz said, "Wait a minute. Look, Hatsky. You know me. I come along after you quit the ring. Is that right? I never wrote a lousy line about you in my life. Is that right?"

"What if it is?" Hatsky said.

Lenz said, "All right, then. Would I steer you wrong?"

"You a boxing writer, isn't it?" Hatsky said to him. He shook his head at the wonderment of it all, at the density of these writers. "Don't you understand? Any of you, don't you understand? This is a important fight. A unusual opportunity for this fighter. Why you want to wreck him like this? What's the matter with you people all of a sudden?"

"Hatsky," Lenz said patiently, "did it ever occur to you that what we're telling you is the truth?"

Hatsky Gideon nodded heavily. "So it's true. If it's true it'd wreck him all the same, wouldn't it?" He looked challengingly about. "Wouldn't it?"

The writers said nothing.

"If it's true," Hatsky said in his tongue-heavy voice, "he can't do nothing about it nohow, can he?"

Lenz said gently, "He's got to know, Hatsky."

"Not now, he don't," Hatsky said.

"What do you mean, not now?"

"He's got to fight, don't he? Right now I wouldn't tell him if it was my own mother." Hatsky shook his head. "That's a awful thing to say, but if it was my own mother I wouldn't tell that boy."

"Hatsky," Lenz said, "look at it this . . ."

"If it was true he couldn't do nothing about it nohow," Hatsky repeated thickly, and there was a dogged degree of truth to what he said that aggravated the newsmen all the more.

"This thick puncho can't get it through his head," one of the writers said. "You can't get through to him."

"An addlepate," one of the others said profoundly.

Hatsky Gideon said darkly, "I'll show you who's a alpate."

"The hell with it," Lenz said. "The fighter doesn't know, but we do. It's all I'm going to need for now."

He turned and headed back for the arena, and, after a moment's indecision, the others flocked after him.

At ringside, Lenz squirmed his way back into his seat and ran some copy paper into his typewriter and, using only the lower-case letters on the keyboard as was his habit, wrote:

npr collect
gpa/ny
bulletin matter plane
    less than ten minutes before the bout was due to
start it was established that webber's wife and daughter were on the plane. however, a guard stationed

outside the boxer's dressing room refused to permit the news to reach him.

lenz saint nick

Perhaps in the days before Brooklyn lost its only daily newspaper, the wedding of Jim Laurie and Lena Kramer would have commanded at least a paid notice if nothing else; but nowadays nobody had thought of it, least of all the parents of the happy pair, who had their own troubles. At the wedding ten days ago, somebody—somebody's drunk Aunt Rhoda or black-sheep Uncle Kenneth —had suggested that there was no reason for in-laws not to get to know each other right along with the newlyweds; and somebody else had raised a toast to the Tuesday Night Club, which was an old people's social institution in the neighborhood; and it had seemed the most natural thing in the world for the Lauries and the Kramers to decide on a Tuesday Night Club for themselves. This was the second Tuesday night since the wedding—last Tuesday, the Kramers, parents of the bride, had visited the Lauries, and this Tuesday, the Lauries, parents of the groom, were visiting the Kramers.

And already each couple was looking for the opportunity to beg off the following Tuesday.

Mr. Laurie was a carpenter and Mr. Kramer was in the fur business, and they did not understand each other. The two men both liked poker, but their wives did not. Last Tuesday night they had settled for an evening of television, and this Tuesday night, after some small amount of talk about it, they were settling for an evening of television. Mrs. Kramer made popcorn, and there was a good deal of talk about the honeymoon (now about to end), though the jokes had not yet reached an equal level on both sides, so that while Mr. Laurie was laughing very hard, Mr. Kramer did not laugh at all.

At nine o'clock, Mr. Laurie was telling the one about the bride sliding down the balustrade; then, upon a small laugh, he launched into the one about the bandleader and the bridegroom. And between the jokes and some additional false ceremony about the popcorn, the four of them heard the announcement on TV at nine o'clock, but not very well. And when Mr. Kramer put up his hand and said, "Wait! What's he saying?" gesturing toward the TV set, they caught only the tail end of the bulletin.

First there was an argument between Mr. and Mrs. Kramer about Mrs. Kramer's fat mouth, by which Mr. Kramer meant, as politely as he could, to include the fat mouths also of Mr. and Mrs. Laurie, especially Mr.'s; then there was the customary chorus of "It couldn't be them," and Mrs. Kramer went and got the telegram she had received from her daughter Lena (she said it was from Lena, though it was signed by groom as well as bride).

"Everybody, I'll read you what Lena said," Mrs. Kramer said. "I'll read it slow."

"Read every word," her husband advised in a sinister voice. "Don't miss anything."

"Everything but the Western Union part that don't mean anything," Mrs. Kramer said.

"Leave out the collect part too if you want," Mr. Kramer said, and gazed momentarily at the parents of the sponger his daughter had married.

"Just the message," Mrs. Kramer said, and cleared her throat.

FLYING HOME TONIGHT. WILL GO STRAIGHT TO
APARTMENT. IS IT READY? WILL PHONE TOMORROW.
HONEYMOON WONDERFUL.

"And it's signed—" she cleared her throat again, as if she were about to introduce trumpeted spirits—"Lena and Jim."

"Let me see that," Mr. Kramer said, and took the telegram from her and read it over. Mr. Laurie, not quite so tall, raised himself on tiptoe so he could read it over Mr. Kramer's shoulder.

Mr. Kramer read it thoroughly and then handed it to Mr. Laurie, who for some reason remained on tiptoe to read it through once more by himself. Then Mr. Laurie rocked to rest upon his heels and said, "What do you think?"

"Sixteen words," Mr. Kramer said. Everyone understood that he did not say this in any venal sense. He had merely counted the words, and now, having counted them, was reciting a known statistic, a statistic that everyone in the room could verify; and in moments of doubt and impending disaster, there is hardly anything else so comforting.

"Phone the *Daily News*," Mrs. Kramer said.

"Now just hold on to yourselves and wait a minute, everybody," Mr. Laurie said. "Don't get excited."

"What airline did it say?" Mrs. Laurie said.

"It didn't," Mr. Laurie said.

"I don't mean the telegram. The television."

"I didn't hear," Mr. Kramer said pointedly. "Frieda was making noise."

"We got a telegram at home," Mr. Laurie said. He turned to his wife. "What did it say?"

"It didn't say," Mrs. Laurie said.

"Did it say the airline?" Mr. Kramer said.

"We left it home," Mr. Laurie said.

"I think it was the same telegram," Mrs. Laurie said, "except it was signed Jim and Lena instead of Lena and Jim."

The real sense of true danger had not yet penetrated. It was too unlikely; the chances were too much against it. There was a half-hour mystery program on the television now, and occasionally one of the four people in the room turned to stare hard at the screen, as if that would bring forth a bulletin that would say the plane was not from Miami at all.

"I think maybe they may have taken off from Miami *Beach*," Mr. Kramer said.

"They got no airport at Miami Beach," Mr. Laurie said.

"But they were staying at Miami Beach," Mr. Kramer said.

"They'd still leave from Miami."

"I kept telling them," Mr. Kramer said. "If I told them once, I told them a hundred times. Don't take the same plane. When you fly someplace together, go on separate planes. Isn't that what I said?"

"He begged them," Mrs. Kramer said to Mr. and Mrs. Laurie.

"Don't go on the same plane," Mr. Laurie repeated, a little bitterly. "It's a honeymoon. You know what happens on a honeymoon? You got any idea?"

"Who went to Sea Gate on his honeymoon?" Mr. Kramer said. "What are you asking me, I got any idea what happens when it's two people on a honeymoon?"

"Especially a boy and a girl," Mrs. Kramer said.

"All right, then," Mr. Laurie said. "How can you tell them don't go on the same plane?"

"In my business," Mr. Kramer said to Mr. Laurie, using his hands as he talked, "executives of the same corporation never take the same plane. They go to a sales meeting, a convention, an inspection for a new plant—anyplace they fly together they fly separate." Mr. Kramer's index finger began to wag. "You know why?"

"Why?" Mr. Laurie said.

"Because things happen, that's why," Mr. Kramer said. "Because they're too valuable, those men."

"They're no more valuable than my son," Mr. Laurie said.

"Or my daughter," Mr. Kramer said quickly. He began to pace the floor. "Certainly no more valuable."

"In fact, less valuable," Mr. Laurie said.

"Less valuable," Mr. Kramer agreed. "And yet a lousy stinking business firm—a company without a soul—this company will do this much for its executives. What do we do for our children? Ah." He uttered a short, hoarse laugh. "Different, hey? Because it's their honeymoon, now we say to them, 'You are less valuable than the brass of some company someplace, so while they take different planes, you will take the same plane.'"

"Less valuable," Mr. Laurie said again. "The corporation men are less valuable."

"I just finished saying that," Mr. Kramer said, and stopped to look at the other man.

"In fact, they're not valuable at all, those corporation executives," Mr. Laurie said. "They make them take separate planes, why? Not because they care if any one of them lives or dies but because it would be inconvenient for more

71

than one of them to die at the same time. They would have trouble readjusting at the home office. The loss of one—all right. This they don't mind. Why should they? That they can write off. But the loss of more than one—oh, no. This makes it harder."

Mr. Kramer said, "Your point is not clear to me."

"My point," Mr. Laurie said, standing before the other man and looking up at him, "is simply this, and I quote myself: If you worry about what can happen to you when you fly, then you shouldn't fly at all."

"You're not worried about the children?" Mr. Kramer said challengingly.

"I'm—"

"You're not worried about your own son? Never mind my daughter for a minute. But your own son?"

"I—"

"Flesh of your flesh?" Mr. Kramer said.

"Let him talk," Mrs. Kramer said to Mr. Kramer.

"What for?" Mrs. Laurie said. "All he's got is theories. Some fine theories, I must say."

"I'm worried now, yes," Mr. Laurie said. "But I wasn't before. When they said they were going to fly, so they could have the most time in Florida together, what did I say? I said all right, fly. If I was worried, then I wouldn't have said take separate planes. If I was worried, I would have said do me a favor, don't fly. If they took separate planes, it would have doubled the number of planes something could have gone wrong with." His voice was heaving and almost broken. "That's all it would have done. It wouldn't have lessened the chances any of something going wrong with one plane. A plane that gets something wrong with it is a machine. It don't know how many people are riding inside."

"You don't think," Mr. Kramer said to him, "that the chances of something going wrong with two planes are less than the chances of something going wrong with one plane?"

"I don't think about it, period," Mr. Laurie said defensively. "If before I myself—" he placed a hand over his heart—"or someone dear to me was ready to take a plane I had to stop and ask myself let's split them up and put them on nine different planes, they'll be safer that way; if I had to ask myself that, then what could I do? I could only come up with one answer: Don't fly at all. That's the way I think."

"But you didn't tell them don't fly at all."

"No."

"But you said that was the way you think."

"The other way from that is the way I think."

"Let me ask you something," Mr. Kramer said. "You look like a bright fella. You got insurance?"

"A question, have I got insurance," Mr. Laurie said. "Sure I got insurance." He placed his hand to his heart once again. "The Equitable."

"If you drop dead here right at my feet, half a minute from now, the insurance will pay off?"

"What do you think, sure it'll pay off," Mr. Laurie said.

"All right," Mr. Kramer said. His eyes narrowed. "You going to drop dead now this very minute?"

"God forbid," Mr. Laurie said.

"Then why you got insurance?" Mr. Kramer said.

"Listen," Mr. Laurie said, "you were worried about this?"

"Who?" Mr. Kramer said. "Worried? Me? Do I look worried? Ha!" He flattened his palms together like a diver. "I'm ready to go out the window, he says am I worried."

"All right," Mr. Laurie said to him. "Then I'm going to

tell you something. You committed a crime, that's what you did, that's what I'm going to tell you. If you think the way you do, it was your duty to say to those kids, 'Look!' " He pointed a dramatic finger. " 'Planes isn't safe! Stay on the ground!' That's what it was your duty to say!"

"No," Mr. Kramer said. "No, no, no, no, no. You take out insurance, why? Because you think you're going to drop dead tomorrow? Of course not! Because you want to play it a little safe, that's all. So two people are going to take a plane, all right. So it shouldn't be a total loss, take two planes. That's all. Don't try hang this on me."

"I'm only trying make a little sense out of you," Mr. Laurie said. He fished a quarter from his pants pocket. "Look at this quarter. You throw it up in the air. You might get heads, you might get tails. Right?"

"So he's throwing a quarter," Mr. Kramer said. "What it has to do with anything, don't ask."

"I'm trying to show you something," Mr. Laurie said. "If you went up to an insurance man and said to him, 'How do you do, sir, I am going to take ten thousand plane trips, please insure me,' why, the insurance man would break his back laughing. Such a policy you'd get for this. *But*—if you already took nine thousand nine hundred ninety-nine plane trips, you say please insure me for number ten thousand, what would you get? The regular insurance, that's what. I tell you I'm going to throw heads with this quarter ten thousand times in a row, you tie yourself up laughing. But if I throw nine thousand nine hundred ninety-nine heads, what's the odds on ten thousand? Still the same as they was on number one. The quarter don't know. The quarter's got a brain inside it, it knows how many times it was thrown up in the air?"

Mr. Kramer threw up his hands. "So we're throwing a quarter for heads and tails?"

"I mean a plane crashes, it crashes."

"That's a nice sentiment."

"Let me put it this way to you," Mr. Laurie said. "You say they should have took two planes instead of one."

"Yes."

"All right. So under your system tonight we lose one kid instead of two. Which one?"

Mrs. Laurie, seated on the sofa, gave a moan and began to rock, hugging herself and weeping.

"It's not even sure it's their plane," Mrs. Kramer said to her. She went to the sofa to comfort the other woman, and then she too began to cry, silently, her face working and wrinkled; and she reached aimlessly for a handkerchief. "It's not them," she gasped at last. "It's not them."

"A hundred to one shot it isn't any trouble for those two," Mr. Kramer said.

"It's better than a hundred to one," Mr. Laurie said.

"Here he is talking figures again," Mr. Kramer said.

They forgot all about calling the newspaper. Instead, the two men stood there arguing; the two women stayed, each alone by herself, at opposite ends of the sofa. And at 9:30, when the voice of the television announcer said, "We take you now to our newsroom for a special bulletin," the room became absolutely quiet, and they listened. They listened, but none looked at the TV set.

The announcer gave the news and then the passenger list.

When he said, "Mr. and Mrs. James Laurie of Brooklyn, New York," Mrs. Laurie screamed and fell upon the seat of the sofa. Her husband said, in a loud voice, "Ah! Ah!

75

Ah!" and went to her, falling on his knees beside her.

Mr. Kramer shook his head, again and again, and went to the window and saw that outside the rain was beginning to fall more heavily. He turned back and said to Mr. Laurie, "We were both right. I don't blame you. I was right, they should have taken two planes. You were right, you didn't tell them what to do." He shook his head. "They're kids. What do they listen to what we tell them?"

"Nothing," Mr. Laurie murmured.

"Kids," Mr. Kramer said. "How long ago? Not very. Make it a diaper. Babies."

"Nothing," Mr. Laurie said.

"Whatever you say, they know better," Mr. Kramer said.

And Mrs. Kramer, meanwhile, held out the telegram in her hand and said, in a shocked yet almost conversational tone of voice, "No, it's still not right. It's wrong. It's not them. In the telegram they want to know is the apartment ready? It's ready. It's ready for them. It's waiting. I had the girl there today to clean, myself I went over it with her, every corner of the apartment, the foyer, everything. It isn't my Lena and her boy. They asked in the telegram was the apartment ready, all they have to know is it's ready. And in the morning . . ." She was talking completely to herself, yet talking loudly none the less ". . . they'll call up. Like they said they would. Hello."

MARSHALL KENT, the vice-president of Coastal Airlines, said, "God damn it, God damn it, God damn it."

"How is your head?" Felix Allerdyce, the advertising man, said to him.

"What kind of a question is that, how's my head?" Kent said.

Allerdyce consulted his watch. It was 9:30. His pill commercial would be on now. "Here," he said. "Look at this. Here's the pill I was telling you about."

Kent looked, like a cougar at bay.

The TV came into focus and the announcer said, "We take you now to our newsroom for a special bulletin."

The two men watched and listened, saying nothing. After the news bulletin, the station went over to its next program direct, without any station-break commercials.

Marshall Kent said, "That's what you call your pill?"

"I'm sorry," Allerdyce said. "I can't control this kind of thing."

"Lovely," Kent said. "Lovely, lovely. You're all alike, aren't you? Sons-of-bitches, every one of you."

Allerdyce took a pull at his drink. He said, "Were you addressing me?"

"No," Kent said, "I was talking to J. Edgar Hoover."

"Marshall," Allerdyce said, "what did I do?"

"Advertising, public relations, newspapermen," Kent said. "They're all the goddam same."

"I've never been in the newspaper business in my life," Felix Allerdyce said.

Kent ignored him. "Some hotshot newspaperman got ahold of this. What's his name? Called me on the phone half hour ago. Gammon." He thought for a moment. "Gammon. Now, tell me one thing. Who told him?"

"Well, to tell you the truth, I don't know," Allerdyce said.

"I don't know," Kent said in mirthless mimicry. "I don't know. You're all alike, you bastards. Every one of you."

"Marshall," Felix Allerdyce said, "why are you mad at me?"

"Because," Kent said, "all you pimps are the same. Get something people will read or listen to. That's what you're in business for. Newspapermen, ad men, press agents. All the same."

"But," Allerdyce said, "people like you depend on people like us."

"That's right," Kent said heavily. "That's right, we do. And look where it gets us."

"But it wasn't a newspaperman who crashed your plane for you," Allerdyce said.

"You see?" Kent said to him. "You're even talking like one now."

"What do you mean?"

"Who said the plane was crashed?"

"Well," Allerdyce said, "I assumed . . ."

"Eighty million people assuming the same damn thing by now," Kent said. "Freedom of the goddam press."

ACROSS THE WAY from Albie Webber's dressing room at St. Nicholas Arena, his opponent of the evening, Wolf Hagan, was preparing for the ten-round main event in an atmosphere dedicated to relaxation. Wolf wanted his back rubbed? The *small* of the back? Dolphin Grimes, his second, was the best back-rubber in the business; specialty: the *small* of the back. Wolf wanted to hear the baseball scores? Marc Klein, the other second, would run the scores back from the press row at ringside. Wolf wanted music on the radio? Happy Gallant, his manager, had brought a radio with him.

At 9:30, half an hour before fight time, the music on the radio went off and the announcer cut in with the bulletin about the plane, together with the passenger list.

Wolf Hagan was lying on the rubbing table, but when he heard that Mrs. Albie Webber of Tenafly, New Jersey, was on the plane, together with her five-year-old daughter Jane, he sat bolt upright.

"That's the ball game," he said.

"Whatsamatta?" Happy Gallant said, and added as an aside to Dolphin Grimes, "*Rub* him, damnit. *Rub* him!"

"Fight's off," Hagan said.

Happy Gallant said, "What'd he say?"

"He said fight's off," Dolphin Grimes said.

"You shaddap," Gallant said to Grimes. He turned to the fighter. "Lie down."

"I ain't gonna fight him," Hagan said.

"Will you stop this all of a sudden?" his manager said. "Rub the back, Dolphin, what's the matter with you?"

"You got ears, ain't you?" Hagan demanded.

"Oh, I got ears," the manager said. "Look at me, I got ears. I'm Miss America, is who." He minched his way across the dressing room while Dolphin and Wolf Hagan stared at him. "There she is," Gallant sang, "Miss A-MER-ica. Oh, yes. I just beat out Miss Kentucky, *and* Miss Wisconsin, *and* Miss Ioway. Why? 'Cause I got ears. I'm a hot sexy babe, I am. All right, boys. Line forms on the right. Smoking in the balcony. Who's first? Miss America, right here, ready and waiting. Com-plete down to the ears."

"That's his wife and the kid," Hagan said.

"Who told you?" the manager said.

"I got ears."

"Oh, you got ears too," Happy Gallant said. "Three big

whizbang cheers for you. Oh ree rah. Oh ree rah. Oh ree rah." He began to sing again. "I got ears, you got ears, all Gods' chillun got ears. When I get to hebbin gonna . . ."

"Listen to me," Hagan said.

Gallant continued to sing, ". . . cut off dem ears an' gonna walk all over God's hebbin!"

"Boom!" Dolphin Grimes echoed.

"Hebbin!" Gallant sang.

"Boom!" sang Grimes.

"HEBBIN!" Gallant cried.

"Stop the———," Wolf Hagan, the fighter, said. He put his hand against his eyes. "I don't want to hear that kind of———any more."

"Whatsamatta with you all of a sudden?" Happy Gallant said to him. "What—sa—matta? You want to hear the odds? You eight to five, old buddy." He put his hands before him in a gesture that swore to heaven. "Did I ever tell you a lie when I told you what was the odds? Did I? When I tell you eight to five, what I'm saying is don't worry, that's what I'm saying."

Hagan pointed toward the radio. "Didn't you hear? His wife and his kid are on the plane!"

"Did he say it was the wife and the kid of Albie Webber the fighter? For sure did he say that?"

"Listen," Hagan said, "how many Albie Webbers you think there are in this world?"

"Maybe offhand six hundred thousand," Gallant said. "Maybe more. I dunno. Dolphin, I told you rub him."

"Six hundred thousand Albie Webbers!" Hagan said. "Six hundred thousand Albie Webbers!" He began to nod his head profoundly. "And all six hundred thousand of these is from Tenafly, New Jersey. Imagine this."

"Webber ain't from Tenafly," Gallant said.

"No?"

"He only says that. I know him from the East Side."

"Me too," Dolphin Grimes said.

"See?" Gallant said to Wolf Hagan.

"If he says he's from Tenafly it's the same thing as being from Tenafly," Hagan said. "What're you trying to give me? What do I look? Dumb?"

"All I'm saying is don't believe everything you hear off of the radio," Gallant said.

"The announcer said," the fighter said.

"The announcer said," the manager said. "The announcer happens to be a liar. He was born a liar and he'll die a liar."

Wolf Hagan looked at him and moistened his lips. "Why would he lie about something like that?"

"Born liars lie about anything," the manager said. "That right, Dolphin?"

"The truth ain't in him," Dolphin said.

The other second, Marc Klein, poked his head in the door and said, "Hey, Wolf. Cardinals get three in the third."

"Get the ——— out of here," the fighter said to him.

"I'll check the Orioles for you," Klein said.

Wolf Hagan said something remarkably unpleasant about the Orioles, and Klein shrugged helplessly and went out again.

"And if it *was* him, so what?" Happy Gallant said to the fighter. "Suppose it is his wife and kid. Take a one-in-a-thousand shot and suppose it is. What difference does it make? What is this business with you all of a sudden, stop the fight? What are you talking?"

"Look, you're my manager," Wolf Hagan said to him.

"Sure," Gallant said. "I got the license. I was banned in

Massachusetts for a while, but I got it fixed before the NBA made it universal. I'm all right. I'm your manager. Now what?"

"I got a wife and kid myself," the fighter said.

"I didn't say you didn't."

"They get killed on an airplane, what am I going to do?"

"I don't know. They ain't on an airplane. They're home where they're supposed to be."

"What I'm trying to say, I know how that other man feels," Hagan said. "I know what Albie Webber's going to do."

"All right, you tell me," Happy Gallant said to his fighter. "What's Albie Webber going to do?"

"He's going to do the only thing he can do, because he can't do anything else," Hagan said. "He can't do nothing about the plane, there's nothing he can do, so he's going to do the only thing he can."

"And what's that?"

Hagan slid off the table and stood up, alone by himself. "He's going to get in that ring and take it out on me. He's going to kill me."

IT WAS 9:57 P.M.

On an ordinary flight, Coastal 214 would be past the half-way mark in its journey to New York.

At this point, traditionally, reliable word would be at hand at LaGuardia as to a probable arrival time. Once in a while, people meeting the plane would get to the airport as early as now. Having nothing else to do with their evening, they would kill time by wandering the observation platform, watching other planes take off and land.

By 9:45, the flight counter flanking the waiting room in one of the two passenger-staging wings downstairs would have accurate word and would chalk up the plane's ETA on the board.

At 9:57, Louis Reagan, on duty for Coastal behind the baggage counter, ducked out for a moment and went in to the Operations Office.

He was back at 9:59.

Coastal's operations into LaGuardia were limited to the point where the airline shared this particular passenger section with another carrier. Reagan could not tell whether the people waiting around outside the counter were concerned with Coastal 214 or with flights belonging to the other line.

He wanted to be inconspicuous about it, but there was no other way he could handle it.

He stepped swiftly to the whiteboard behind the counter. On the board were listed Coastal's four Miami inbounds, and the same number of outbounds—eight flight movements a day. The two flights of nearest import at this time were 214, due to arrive at 11:45 P.M., and 107, due to depart at 3:30 A.M.

Next to 214, under the heading WILL ARRIVE, where the actual arrival time was to be posted, Reagan hesitated for a moment, then printed one word: *Indefinite*.

He didn't know what to do about 107, due to leave at 3:30 in the morning. Airplanes, Reagan knew, do not grow on trees.

And 107 was supposed to be the Everyinch too.

Turning a plane around in New York was a simple job for Coastal Airlines. Every one that came in turned around and went back to Miami, and that was that. If the arrival of one was late, the departure of the same would be put back as necessary. Things were considerably more complicated at the Miami end. It was set up so that five planes were assigned to handle the four daily Miami–New York round trips, but those five were not necessarily the same planes each day. A plane that arrived in Miami from New York at noon, with the next New York–bound flight scheduled for four o'clock in the afternoon, earned no money sitting on the ground for four hours. It could be serviced and fueled and routed to Cincinnati within two hours. Then an incoming flight from Texas could in its turn become the four o'clock flight to New York. To say, therefore, that Coastal rotated five planes for the four New York trips was actually to use a manner of speaking that allowed, as a general rule, for one extra available four-engine craft on the ground at Miami at most times. Miami being an important terminus for the line, this was necessary; the CAB frowned on airlines that could not meet their own approved schedules.

It was an immensely complicated picture, the field of traffic management, illustrated perhaps by the fact that American Airlines, biggest of the domestic carriers, could fly hundreds of regularly scheduled flights each day, as well as frequent special flights and added holiday movements, with only some eighty planes, a certain number of which were always on the ground for periodic inspection and servicing. By comparison, the job of train dispatcher at the height of the Grand Central rush hour was a pleasure. You had so many tracks, and if anything went wrong on one track, nothing would be able to move on that track till the trouble was cleared up. Additional equipment could be secured readily. Your engineers did not work for an outfit where, at the end of a typical work day, they might find themselves in Honolulu.

Most of all, though, the problem related itself to weather.

Of special bearing, within this problem, was the fact that an aircraft had been reported in trouble.

In New York now, as it rained, there was no wind. La-Guardia's ceiling spot outlined the lower base of clouds over the airport, and the base was more than 1,000 feet from the ground. For the past hour or more, operations had been handled westbound on the main east-west runway, which brought planes in over the water, and Flushing Meadow before that; and took them off into the west, whither most of them were traveling anyway.

With no wind to speak of, the routine could have been shifted to northbound on the north-south runway, where the beam approach setup was, but so long as the wind stayed away and the ceiling stayed up there was no need to make the change.

Within six hours, Weather said, the winds could be expected to freshen. The rain was a steady one.

Not that the 10 P.M. weather in New York made any difference to Coastal 214. But the point was that in reacting to the emergency, the talents of the CAA, in charge of Air Traffic Control, had to deal at the same time with the fact that the emergency had not only to be met but, also, to be kept from spreading. It was of little importance in this respect whether Coastal 214 was down in the ocean somewhere or, by some unlikely quirk, still flying. To be sure, a plane in trouble on a heavily-traveled airway was a menace to other planes, but the chance of mid-air collision was practically nonexistent . . . at this stage anyway. It was part of the general safety picture simply to keep the flow of information and the check-in times of other planes on a normal and routine basis. It was part of the general safety picture to try to disrupt timetables as little as possible. A plane from Miami to Washington could as a conceivable example have three connecting flights originating at Washington and waiting on the ground there, and if weather moved in while they were waiting, then a decision would have to be made as to whether they could take off at all. A disruption in schedules went farther—it was the easiest way to cause a tight situation over some destination field where planes began coming in faster than the tower could land them; let alone the question of whether the airport had sufficient apron space on the ground. Then the planes would be stacked, and if to a stack caused by traffic you were to add a stack caused by weather, there would be planes backed up in the sky to the point where at least one might, in his circling, run low on fuel, and then somehow you would have to pick that one man out of the stack and land him and hope that nothing went wrong. At times like these you might remember, perhaps ruefully, perhaps gratefully, that God packed a lot of room in three dimensions. Casey Jones and the *Andrea Doria* could have used that extra room.

So you ran the business of guiding aircraft through the skies on as routine a basis as you could, because of, as well as in spite of, the unscheduled misfortune of one of their number. And hysteria was kept at a minimum—except in the one case tonight of the Everyinch. Marshall Kent, vice-president of Coastal Airlines, may indeed have had a point.

Some form of damage, perhaps many more forms than one, could be produced by telling too many too early too much. Too much could, in fact, be too little.

One example was the way the news agencies jumped on the fact that the plane following Coastal 214 carried 91 persons. Immediate reference was made to the Grand Canyon crash of June 30, 1956, when two eastbound giants, having taken off from Los Angeles only three minutes apart, collided and crashed, bringing death to 128 persons.

They should have stopped to reason that such a thing could not happen here, because there were two salient differences between tonight's flights and those of the Canyon disaster. One difference was that in this case both aircraft were headed for the same destination—New York nonstop—which meant they had carefully been assigned noticeably different flight routes at the outset. Another difference was that neither of tonight's planes was on visual flight plan. Both were flying an instrument-controlled, radar-watched airway.

ATC in Jacksonville, too, had of course ordered the following plane even higher and wider of the Everyinch's path than the original plan had called for, as soon as the Everyinch first failed to report.

And, most encouraging of all from this particular standpoint, there soon ceased to be any indication that the Everyinch was in the air at all.

Nonetheless, news could travel faster than aircraft, and rumor could travel faster than news.

So there was all of this. And at the check-in counter for Coastal Airlines at LaGuardia, Louis Reagan, having posted the word *Indefinite* opposite the inbound 214, shrugged and went ahead and wrote *Canceled* opposite the outbound 107.

Nᴏᴛ ʟᴏɴɢ ᴀfᴛᴇʀ ten o'clock, Emmy Verdon heard again from Willard Trace. What he said confirmed only what had been expected, yet it was the knell that had been hoped against, against hope itself.

Now it tolled.

A message had been received.

ATC no longer had Coastal 214 on radar.

There had been a change in Emmy in the past hour. She had become less distant toward Ben Gammon, more willing to talk, and she had talked at length about herself and about the times she and Mike Trace had had together. There was no tracing what had brought about this change in her, marked though it was—it might have been in the main the instinct of one human being to fall back upon another, to warm to the other, in the face of danger. Perhaps it is even true that when the danger is not shared equally by the two, the reliance of the first person upon the second becomes the more pronounced.

Now she hung up the phone, and Gammon said to her, "Willard?"

She nodded and stood there by the phone for a moment.

Ben Gammon said, "Plane down?"

She nodded again.

"What'd he say?"

"They don't see it on radar any more." Emmy's voice was low but controlled.

"When did they lose him?"

"I don't know." Emmy moved away from the phone, as much as anything in a gesture that told Gammon it was his to use to get in touch with his office.

And there had been a change in Gammon too. Up till now, he had had, if he would have admitted it, a sense, in phoning the first bulletins to his news agency, of vicarious participation in an event of great danger and urgency and moment. Now, though, he picked up the receiver tiredly and not a little sorrowfully. He called his office duty-bound.

When he was through, he took out his wallet and extracted his press card; stared at it for a long moment, then turned and sent it sailing across the room in a wicked arc.

"What the hell is it for?" he muttered. "I didn't even know that man."

Emmy said, "What man?"

"What's his name?—Kent. Never heard of him till to-night. But I'm a newspaperman. I've got a press card. I can call him up and ask him questions and threaten him and every other damn thing. Did you ever think what kind of stupid rights and powers they give to reporters? A doctor, a lawyer, an architect, a plumber—they've all got to have licenses; they've got to pass exams. What do you have to do to be a newspaperman? Go to journalism school someplace? The worst thing you can do if you're looking for a job in the newspaper business is show a diploma from a journalism school. Down at Global Press we've got a special door we throw those guys out of."

Emmy said, "It's your job."

He nodded. "It's my job. They give me a press card, I can pry into anything I want."

"Do you think they're alive in the ocean?" Emmy said.

"I don't know," he said. "I don't know why not."

Harrison, in Coastal Cargo at LaGuardia, had a call put through to him. It was from a woman. She introduced herself as Mrs. Cameron Fletcher III. She said "the Third," and you could see the "III" hung up as if finger-painted in the air, the way she said it.

"My champion is on that plane," Mrs. Fletcher said.

"What plane?" Harrison said. He knew what plane.

"Your flight two hundred and fourteen," Mrs. Fletcher said. "What do you propose to do about it?"

"Who'd you say was on it?" Harrison said.

"My champion," Mrs. Fletcher said.

"Who's your champion?"

"Champion Venerable Lady Standaright of Locust Farm."

"Ah," Harrison said.

"Best bitch at Westport two years running," Mrs. Fletcher said. "What do you propose to do about it? I ask you again."

"Lady, I'm a son-of-a-bitch if I know," Harrison said. "We got enough troubles around here. Believe me."

"Young man," Mrs. Fletcher said over the telephone, "in addition to everything else I intend to report you for your language."

"Lady," Harrison said, "what is it you're trying to tell me? Believe me, we got problems here all of a sudden."

"My dog," Mrs. Fletcher said. "My dog, young man."

"The insurance on it?"

"Never mind the insurance. A dog's life is at stake."

"I hear they got some human lives at stake too," Harrison said.

"But not so important as my dog's."

"Really, lady," Harrison said, "when you . . ."

90

"The people are on there because of choice," Mrs. Fletcher said, "with the exception perhaps of the very young children. My dog had no choice in the matter. She is indeed the supreme innocent being on board that plane. I shall expect her to be saved first, or second at the very latest."

COAST GUARD was alerted at Jacksonville, Savannah, Charleston and Wilmington, North Carolina. The Everyinch was presumed to be down at sea, though in what shape no one knew. The ocean was not friendly tonight—it had picked up a swell in advance of the hurricane.

The Everyinch could be more than a hundred miles offshore, and because it would disappear beneath the lip of radar screens before it actually hit the water, its north-south location could only be guessed at.

One interesting fact had come out, but it was difficult to translate. Three different radar installations, two of them military, had reported losing the plane from their screens. All three reported, however, that the loss occurred at different times—minutes only, but different enough to cause some thinking about it. Each was a different-range set, so that it was possible that their effective base altitudes were different enough for the plane to fall off one screen at a time. There were other possibilities, among them the canceling factor that the independent radar reports might have been in error as to the way they reported the time elements. Indeed, the plane possibly might have gone down into the sea in one long glide path of a hundred miles or more.

At any rate, the public was not the only privileged body in the case of Coastal 214. Because the plane was in the sensitive defense area off the Atlantic seaboard, the military, all the way to the air defense center in Battle Creek, was watching this one.

But at the moment this did not add to the chances for an effective rescue operation. Because of the curve of the mainland, a flight course that would place the plane 150 miles to seaward of Jacksonville could in the same straight line put it no more than 25 or 30 miles offshore of Wilmington; the same path, projected further north, would, no more than 40 miles north of Wilmington, put the Everyinch over land!

But that was extremely unlikely; indeed, the crash spot could conceivably even be southeast of Jacksonville; now, where air radar had left off, surface detection would have to take over.

The hope was for radio contact with fishing vessels which had not yet returned to port on the advice of the hurricane warnings. Marine said that five bigger vessels—three freighters, two tankers—were plying the ocean lanes in the pertinent vicinity. All five were equipped with radar. They were an equal hope.

Somebody was going to locate the Everyinch.

It could reasonably be hoped that life raft and life preservers were in use. But in the rain and the lowering murk and the swelling tide, it was now a question of making the contact in time.

ST. NICHOLAS ARENA had been slow to fill, as always, and the result was that a good number of the fans finally on hand to watch the Albie Webber–Wolf Hagan fight had arrived after hearing, one way or another, the 9:30 news bulletins. Those in the arena who knew that Mrs. Albie Webber and her daughter were aboard the missing plane relayed the information quickly to those who did not. They were all fight fans, nothing more, and they had not made the effort that the newspapermen had made to ascertain that this actually was the wife of the fighter. They assumed she was. They were just as right as the newspapermen.

The grapevine worked with magical instancy; within moments, a man in the first row who had heard it from a man in the second row leaned forward and asked one of the writers in the press row. It was confirmed; and the word bounced off the press row and back to the farthest reaches of the arena.

The only insulated man in the house was Albie Webber, the fighter himself. He did not know and no one now would tell him. The ring announcer looked fearfully at him as he called his name, and on the television microphone, the sportscaster who was going to do the blow-by-blow lowered his voice to a pitch of dramatic intensity and said:

"Ladies and gentlemen, you're looking at a fighter whose wife and child are reported aboard that missing aircraft." The speaker paused and breathed heavily. "We don't know for certain that Albie Webber has been told—it's almost a one-hundred-per-cent certainty that he hasn't. He looks calm, he looks composed, he looks to be in control of himself, the same Albie Webber we've seen before, that same pleasing contender from Tenafly. He's the underdog in this fight, ladies and gentlemen, and now in the face of a . . . well, a titanic personal tragedy, what will he do? What would you do?"

The grapevine was a good 95-per-cent effective. Here and there in the crowd could be found an enthusiast who had not listened or would not listen. They alone cheered the fighters when their names were announced. No one else cheered. There was a whispering, instead: a buzzing, gossipy sound.

A hoarse voice sounded from the gallery:

"Go get him, Albie! Take him apart!"

It could not be known whether the voice knew or not about Albie Webber's wife and child.

But it was all the crowd needed.

They came massed suddenly to their feet, roaring Albie Webber on. And the fighter heard them. He seemed to nod his head, and as the first round commenced he came out and drove a right hand hard to the midsection of Wolf Hagan, then a left and a right to the head, and Hagan was down on his hands and knees amid an animal roar that was, in direct translation, the crowd's pity for the other man— the man who had hit him.

Hagan stayed there where he was, and when the referee had counted to ten he came quickly to his feet, looked once at Albie Webber, then grabbed a towel from one of his seconds and settled it over his shoulders and half-vaulted from the ring.

In his dressing room, Hagan sat on the rubbing table and let Dolphin Grimes, his second, cut the gloves off his hands.

Happy Gallant, Hagan's manager, paced the floor like a caged puma. Suddenly he stopped and pointed a savage finger at his fighter.

"Eight to five! You was eight to five!"

"Shut up," Hagan said to him.

"Oh, yeah, shut up!" the manager yelled. "I'm gonna tell you something, bright boy. You tell me shut up, but I'm gonna tell you something. You're lucky that guy had the wife and kid on the airplane. You hear me? Lucky! Because it wasn't they'll feel sorry for him, the commission'd bar you for life. And hold up the ——— purse too! What are you gonna say to that?"

"Shut up," Hagan said.

"Twenty-seven years I'm in this business," Gallant said. "Twenty-seven years."

"Twenty-eight," Dolphin Grimes said.

"Shut up," Gallant said to him. "What did I do? Did I cheat? Yes, yes, I cheated. Did I steal? Yes, yes, I stole. Did I tell a lie? Yes, yes, I lied like a thief. But did I ever tell a man go off the low board? No. Did I ever put a fighter's gloves in water? Did I ever put the stuff on he could get in the other guy's eyes?"

"You did that time in Omaha," Dolphin Grimes said.

"I'm asking you for the last time shut up," Gallant said to him. "No." He tapped himself rapidly on the chest. "I never told a fighter of mine lie down in my life. Tonight what? 'Oh, I can't fight him! He's going to kill me! Kill me, kill me, kill me!' *Kill you?* That man couldn't kill you with a .32 in one hand and a bayonet in the other. He hit you one time, you got on your knees and stayed there. What are you? A Mohammedan? What were you doing? Facing east? Mecca or something?"

Dolphin Grimes said, "I always wondered about that. If they got to face east and face Mecca at the same time what do they do if they live east of Mecca?"

The other second, Marc Klein, said from the corner of the room, "They got a place called East Mecca."

"Shut up the noise around here!" Gallant yelled. He went and stood before his fighter, putting his face close down to Wolf Hagan's. "I'm gonna tell you something, buster,

I'm gonna tell you something. No matter how it works out, his wife and kid are dead or his wife and kid are alive or it wasn't his wife and kid to begin with, you got one of two things gonna happen. Either you threw the fight. Or you didn't throw the fight in which case I can't even get you a rematch, you lost so bad. So either way Webber gets the shot at the title instead of you. You want to know what I estimate? I estimate two million dollars. A million dollars that should have been yours and a million dollars that got no business being his. Bright boy, you went and kicked two million dollars in the ass." He stood back and nodded. "That's a very great arithmetic you got going for you there. Two million dollars. Wings. Out the window. Bye-bye."

"All right," Hagan said to him.

"All right?" the manager said. "All *right?*" He threw his hands up as if he were a holdup victim. "Two million dollars and all he can say is all right."

"Leave me take a shower, will you, please?" the fighter said.

"What for?" Gallant said. "You didn't sweat none."

"Maybe I want to get wet."

"You already got wet." Gallant jerked his thumb toward the arena outside the door. "You went diving. Remember?"

"You gonna kill me with your jokes," Wolf Hagan said.

"I'm gonna kill you with something else besides jokes," Gallant said. He looked at the two seconds, Marc Klein and Dolphin Grimes. "New way to become champion, boys. Put your family on an airplane that falls down someplace. Then all you got to do is look at the other fighter and he falls down too."

"I ain't gonna listen no more," Hagan said.

"—— well told you you ain't gonna listen no more," the manager said. "Or if you do, you ain't gonna be listening to me. You can go get yourself another manager."

"I don't need another manager."

"What you don't need don't figure into it. What I'm thinking of is what I don't need."

"You need me."

"What for? To show me how to lay down? I can go to Macy's and buy a mattress and have the salesgirl show me how."

Dolphin Grimes said, "I always wondered about that. Why is it illegal to remove the tag from the mattress?"

"I done it once," Marc Klein said. "I didn't know it was illegal."

"First thing you know the cops are going to be around here," Grimes told him grimly.

"They ain't gonna be looking for him when they come," Happy Gallant said. "They're gonna be looking for swan boat here. So." He uttered a short, mirthless laugh and gazed relentlessly at Wolf Hagan. "I need you. I need you, hah?"

"You couldn't make a living without me," Hagan said.

"Well, I'm up a pretty —— good creek then," the manager said, "because I can't make one with you either."

"Look, will you, please?" the fighter said. "Tonight was a fluke."

The manager nodded heavily. "Two million dollars."

"Stop it with the two million dollars," Hagan said. "You're always spending money you ain't got."

"I've stopped spending," Gallant said bitterly. "All I know is Webber's gonna be champion where it should have been you."

97

"No, he won't," Wolf Hagan said. "He's gonna quit fighting."

"Who told you? A gypsy?"

"If it was my wife and kid I'd quit fighting," Hagan said.

"I told you before the fight, you still can't get it through your head," Gallant said. "It wasn't your wife and kid."

N<small>EWS</small>, <small>RUMOR</small>, and isolated factors of hysteria worked almost together now, at this stage; yet something else was beginning to happen too.

Here and there, people connected with the event in one way or another began to be puzzled.

Ben Gammon was one of them.

"In a way, it doesn't make sense," he said.

Emmy Verdon said, "What doesn't?"

"Losing radio contact before losing radar contact."

"I don't understand it," Emmy said. "I don't know how those things work. Is it supposed to be the other way around? Are they supposed to lose the radar before the radio?"

"No," Gammon said. "No. It's not which should happen first. The two of them ought to happen at just about the same time."

"Why?" Emmy said.

"I don't know," Gammon said. "I wish I knew more about that kind of thing." He was standing at the window, looking out at the rain, and the glass in his hand was empty. "I'm not very mechanical. Did I ever tell you about my invention to win the war?"

Emmy said from the sofa, "What war?"

"World War Two," the newspaperman said. "I played a very vital role in that war. I was a clerk in the laundry at the Great Lakes Naval Base."

"How old were you when you enlisted?"

"Who enlisted? I was drafted. In those days they were drafting them into the navy too."

Perhaps both of them were thinking that Mike Trace, by comparison, had not waited to be drafted in the Second World War—had enlisted instead. But neither of them said anything about it. Instead, Emmy said, "And what happened?"

"I need another drink."

"No, you don't," she said in a surprisingly strong voice. "Tell me about your invention."

"Oh," he said. "The Mobile F and J."

"The what?"

"The Mobile F and J. Flotsam and Jetsam. It was for submarines. See, when they were being depth-bombed and one of the bombs hit and busted up the submarine, a lot of stuff would float to the top, and that's how the vessel on the surface could tell the sub was done in. After that, they'd quit the depth charges. Can't I have another drink?"

"No."

"Well," Gammon said, "anyway, I got this idea. Why not equip each submarine with a Mobile F and J?" He started to gesture with his hands. "You know, tie it on the side some way or shove it down into a hatch or whatever the hell would be the practical way to do it. Make it a great big collection of nothing—old navy clothes and pieces of pipe and a couple of instrument dials and lots of oil—all made out of stuff that would shoot right to the top when it was released. Then—" he spread his palms—" the minute you got in trouble on the bottom, release the Mobile F & J, and it would all go to the top and make it look like the depth bomb hit you. Oh, I forgot. Make sure you sent up a lot of air bubbles too. That way they'd lay off bombing you and you could get away."

To Emmy, as he talked about his invention, he looked like a little boy. She said, "But, Ben, that sounds like a wonderful idea. What ever happened to it?"

"Nothing."

"Didn't you tell anybody about it?"

"Who are you going to tell in a laundry? Besides, they probably had something like it already."

"I never heard of anything like it."

"I read the other day the Japs did something like that. Maybe we did too."

"But you could have gone to somebody. Just to find out. Somebody would have known."

"Maybe I didn't want to find out." He turned back to the window. "So I didn't tell anybody. Don't make it sound like I was a traitor or something."

"I didn't mean that," she said.

"Anyway," he said—part of the mask had slipped away and he was hastening to restore it—"I was talking about the plane and not being mechanically minded."

"Well, there's still hope," Emmy said. "Don't you think?"

"Sure I do," he said. "If he's down in the water and he's got any kind of lifesaving equipment at all, they're bound to get some kind of a fix on him, even in bad weather. I just don't understand it, which in itself doesn't mean much. Maybe we've got the story a little twisted. Who knows?"

Emmy said, "What do you mean, twisted?"

"I'm not mad at Willard," he said.

"What's being mad at Willard got to do with it?"

"I mean, if he gave you the facts wrong it doesn't have to be his fault."

"But why would Mike's own brother have the facts wrong?"

"Who knows? Something like this, at this stage of it, nobody really knows what the real point-to-point story is. You know."

"But the important thing is there's still hope," Emmy said again.

"That's right," Ben Gammon said, and turned to look at her. He almost said, *You'll wind up marrying Mike yet*, but it would have been a cruel thing to say—at least, at present. A cruel thing to Emmy, and cruel, too, to himself.

AT 10:19 P.M., a new lead from the wires of the Global Press Association:

A FOUR-ENGINE COASTAL AIRLINER WITH 16 PERSONS ABOARD INCLUDING THE WIFE AND CHILD OF BOXING STAR ALBIE WEBBER IS MISSING AND FEARED DOWN AT SEA OFF THE NORTHERN FLORIDA OR CAROLINA COASTS.

WEBBER, WHO HAD NOT YET BEEN INFORMED OF THE NEWS, SCORED A SENSATIONAL ONE-PUNCH KNOCKOUT OVER HEAVILY FAVORED WOLF HAGAN IN THEIR NATIONALLY TELEVISED BOUT FROM NEW YORK'S ST. NICHOLAS ARENA TONIGHT.

BESIDES HIS FIVE-YEAR-OLD DAUGHTER JANE, THREE OTHER CHILDREN, TRAVELING WITH THEIR PARENTS, WERE AMONG THE PASSENGER LIST OF

TWELVE ON THE PLANE WHICH LEFT MIAMI AT 7:36
P.M., EASTERN TIME, HEADED NONSTOP FOR LA-
GUARDIA AIRPORT IN NEW YORK.

COASTAL AIRLINES REPORTED THAT THE PLANE
FAILED TO MAKE A SCHEDULED RADIO CONTACT AT
8:04 P.M. AT FIRST IT WAS REPORTED THAT DESPITE
FAILURE OF ALL EFFORTS TO MAKE RADIO CONTACT,
THE GIANT AIRCRAFT STILL WAS VISIBLE TO RADAR
WATCHERS ON THE GROUND.

HOWEVER, A LATER REPORT STATED THIS WAS NO
LONGER TRUE. THE PLANE WAS EQUIPPED WITH
LIFESAVING OCEAN GEAR IN CASE OF EMERGENCY
OVER WATER, AND OFFICIALS WERE EXPECTED TO OR-
DER AN OCEAN SEARCH OF THE CRASH AREA DESPITE
THE PREHURRICANE RAINS AND HIGH TIDES LASHING
THE ATLANTIC COAST. ANOTHER PLANE, CHARTERED
FOR THE USE OF ARMY SERVICEMEN AND THEIR DE-
PENDENTS, TOOK OFF FOR NEW YORK FROM MIAMI
FOUR MINUTES FOLLOWING THE DEPARTURE OF THE
ILL-FATED COASTAL FLIGHT 214, WITH 91 (REPEAT
91) PERSONS ABOARD, BUT WAS REPORTED TO HAVE
PASSED THE COASTAL PLANE WITHOUT MISHAP.

IN ADDITION TO ITS TWELVE PASSENGERS AND
CREW OF FOUR, COASTAL 214 WAS REPORTED CARRY-
ING AN EXOTIC CARGO OF FREIGHT.

There was more to it than that, of course, but that was
the top to it. Harry Timmons, the rewrite man at GPA in
New York, had rapped it out in a hurry—working so fast
that at least one line was clearly misleading: the one where
he wrote, "three other children, traveling with their parents," making it sound as if there were three other sets of
parents when what he meant was the Diaz family of five—

but he had accomplished the main purpose, which was to get Albie Webber up in the lead. Some fifteen or twenty million persons had watched Webber knock out Wolf Hagan on television, and Webber was, at this point, the story.

The news agencies had not yet learned when the Coast Guard would start moving in on it; nor that a comparison of radar observations at several southern points had, in a matter of only recent minutes, narrowed the potential crash site. Not by much, but "not much" was enough to eliminate five thousand square miles from the search area.

Still, with the lack of contact and the weather, it was going to be difficult indeed. Difficult and, again, puzzling. There were things about it that did not hold right. Maybe it was nothing more than the fact that this kind of accident never parsed easily while it was in the process of happening. The usual kind—the one you didn't hear about till afterward—gave you the benefit at least of a little hindsight and reflection.

The puzzlement was here though. In Washington, two officials connected with the problem talked on the telephone about it. One of them said to the other, "Now tell me just one more thing. Why would any airline go to the trouble of announcing something like this so early?"

"I don't know," the other said. "I just plain don't know."

"I've got a hunch a lot of people are going to be asking that same question before this is over with," the first official said.

"I think you're right," the other said. "It's a good thing Congress isn't in session."

EDWARD F. BELDING, father of Kenneth Belding, the co-pilot of the Everyinch, had not heard the news yet.

His wife had gone to bed early with one of her headaches, and Belding had set up the card table in the living room of their frame house on the hillside in Donora, Pennsylvania. Donora was at the moment famous for Stan Musial and for a noxious smog attack of several years back, but some day it might be famous for Edward F. Belding, too.

Belding had clipped an ad from *Popular Mechanics* magazine, and at the moment he was working, pen in hand and paper spread out over the table, on a final draft of a letter he was writing to a firm of patent attorneys in Washington, D. C. The letter read:

GENTLEMEN:

Have seen your ad in the *Popular Mechanics* and hasten to reply. I have perfected an invention for airplane safety and having a son who is a ~~co-pilot~~ pilot for Coastal Airlines am as you can see more than interested in this subject generally. The idea is taken from the case of submarines in World War II, which as you know had tremendously perfected periscope design. Now in a plane nowadays it is like driving in a convertible, especially the new models Detroit is making which are lower than ever so the poor driver no longer sits up high enough so he can see over certain humps in the road or even around certain corners being higher up therefore having more circle of vision. But they did not make the roads any lower, only the cars, which will cause more accidents. Anyway, you have heard of a blind spot behind you towards the left and right when you drive, and airplanes have this same danger only even more so. Because they are blind overhead and underneath and directly out behind. You read in the papers all the time how two planes each going 700 miles per hour are approaching each other at a rate combined of 1400 miles per hour meaning by the time the pilots see each other they have no time to react but speed is not what causes these accidents and there have never been any commercial or civilian air accidents and maybe no military either though that is classified to a great extent, of planes hitting head on. The danger is planes hitting from the side or behind where both are going the same way but one faster and from a different height, higher or lower. Therefore my invention is like a submarine periscope which the pilot would see behind him and above and below looking into a mirror in the flight cabin. The periscope itself would extend the length of the passenger cabin up against the ceiling for rear view and out of the flight cabin upwards and downwards for upward and downward looking. I know the biggest problem in the flight cabin is space, but my invention would occupy less space than 360 degree radar which would be the real answer, but difficult to perfect and install. Some fighters have had rear radar so a blip shows on the screen when somebody is on their tail but you need more than this. Now, my interest is in patenting and getting some money to . . .

At that point in the letter, the phone rang and somebody told him about Coastal 214.

DUTIFULLY, THE WIFE and son of Herman Jonas had gone with him to the airport to see him off on the Everyinch. The son was seventeen years old, gangling and wary, the product of his mother's first marriage. The mother was a small, bitter-faced woman, with rouge plastered like twin boils on her cheeks.

"You'd think he'd have given me more than thirty-five dollars," she said. "What am I going to do with thirty-five dollars?"

"You married him, old lady," the son said. "Not me."

"What if one of us had to go to the hospital?" she said. They were seated at the kitchen table in the flat-roofed subdivision house that Herman Jonas owned. "What would thirty-five dollars do then?"

"Use his Blue Cross," the son said. "What do you think insurance is for?"

"What's going to happen now?" she said. "You going to start in defending him?"

"Not me," her son said. "All I was saying was simply he's got insurance."

"Has he ever got insurance," the mother said. "Andy, you know what being insurance-poor means?"

"Not exactly," the boy said.

"It means," the mother said, "you spend so much on insurance, you don't have enough left over to afford the everyday things of life. Thirty-five lousy stinking dollars, and he'll be nearly a week in New York. Now do you understand?"

"In other words," the boy, Andy, said in a soft voice, "he's got a lot of insurance."

"But it's life insurance, practically all of it," his mother said. "If something happens with doctors or hospitals, what good does it do?"

"I know," Andy said.

"What do you mean, you know?"

"I know about his life insurance."

"How do you know?"

"I just know."

"Have you been looking through his papers again?"

"Why not? You do it."

"I'm his wife."

"I'm his son."

"No, you're not."

"He keeps telling me I am."

"You're your father's son."

"He keeps telling me treat him like my real father."

"It was a black day I married him," the mother said. Her face worked and she began to cry. "Andy, be a good boy and get me the brandy off the shelf in the cupboard. I only did it for you."

"Cut it out, old lady," the boy said, and went and got the brandy and set the bottle down in front of her.

"A glass too," she said to him. "What do you take your mother for? A barstool slut or something?"

"Maybe I should get two glasses," the boy said.

"How old do you think you are?" she said.

"I'm old enough."

"I'll decide when you're old enough."

"What am I going to drink?"

"Why do you have to drink anything?"

"Well," the son said, "we're sitting here celebrating."

"Huh," the mother said. She took the glass he gave her and poured the brandy for herself. "Celebrating what? These same four walls? The thirty-five dollars?"

"We're celebrating because he's . . ." The boy paused. Then he said, ". . . not here."

The mother nodded. "I didn't think of that." She drank some brandy. "You're right. Go ahead. Pour yourself something."

"Some what?"

"Pepsi-Cola," the mother said.

"Come on," the son said.

"I said Pepsi, I mean Pepsi," the woman said. "What do you think I'm raising my son to be? A pimp or something?"

"Language, old lady. Language," the boy said.

"Thirty-five lousy stinking dollars," she said.

"But," he said, sitting down at the table across from her without pouring himself anything to drink, "there's always the insurance."

"Sure. The insurance. If he drops dead."

"Maybe he will."

"Him? He's healthy as a horse."

"He flies a lot," the boy said.

"That's right," the mother said. "He flies a lot."

"Planes crash sometimes."

"We might as well sit here and dream," she said, and had some more brandy.

"Old lady," the boy said, "do you hate him?"

"Why do you have to ask me that?" she said.

"Tell me," he said. "I want to know. Do you hate him? Do you really hate him?"

She sat there, her hand gripping the glass, staring into emptiness. After a time, she said slowly, "Yes. I hate him. I hate him. Him and his stinking thirty-five lousy dollars."

"I hate him too," the boy said quietly.

The mother nodded. "Pour yourself something and we'll drink to it."

He did not move. Instead, his eyes seemed to come

alight. "And if he crashes on a plane, the insurance is worth more, isn't it?"

"He didn't take out any of that flight insurance at the airport," the mother said. "He was going to, but we were late getting there."

"The regular life insurance he's got ought to be plenty," the boy said.

"All right," she said, a little more thickly and heavily than before. "When's the crash?"

"It'd be all right with you, wouldn't it?" the boy said. He was watching her carefully.

"Listen," she said to him, "I don't care what happens to the son-of-a-bitch so long as I can get my hands on something more than what he's been leaving around."

"Old lady," the son said, "it's a good thing for both of us I'm smart."

She nodded and refilled her glass. "Some day you'll be a famous scientist and give money to your mother."

"That's right," he said, and paused, looking at her. "I'm working on something right now."

"That's my son," she said. "Always studying." She nodded in brandied approval.

Suddenly he stood up. "Back in a minute," he said. "Something to show you."

She nodded again, looking deeply into her glass, and was not aware of the time it took for him to return.

"Here," he said, when he did come back. "See what I've got?"

She looked dimly. "Scrapbooks," she said. "Scrapbooks. Two scrapbooks." She shook her head. "I didn't know you kept scrapbooks."

"Look, old lady," he said, and placed the books down

109

upon the table, then started to run through the pages. "This one was the one that happened in Canada. This other one was the one that happened in Colorado. Both times they put bombs on the planes and blew them up. Both times they were caught."

"What's that?" the woman said. "What's that?"

"They didn't think it through enough," the boy said. "Now, old lady, listen and try to understand. What I've been working on is something entirely different. New in principle. Are you listening?"

She nodded.

"What you do is think with them all the way." He had begun to talk more rapidly. "The investigators, I mean. A bomb blows up a plane, they can figure out later what happened. Why? Because they're looking for it, that's why. They're not miracle men. If they have no other reason for a plane crashing, they look for reasons. But if they have a reason—" he shook his head slowly—"they'll never look any farther." He smiled. "So. You give them a reason. You understand, old lady? You make something else happen first. Before the bomb goes off."

"Something else," the woman said dully, nodding her head.

"It works in three stages," her son said. "The last stage is the bomb going off. The stage before that is something else wrong with the plane—not too bad, not too good. Enough to make them think it's what brought about the crash, but not so much that when they look at it they think of sabotage. The hydraulic . . . well, you don't understand. Anyway, that's stage number two." He smiled. "Stage number one, before anything happens, is for the radio to go dead. So he can't report stage number two to anybody. You see, old lady? You see how it all ties together? It's a problem, old lady, but it deserves being solved, don't you think?"

"I suppose so," the mother said, drinking. "The trouble is, you wouldn't do it."

"No?"

"No. Now that I think of it you're always talking about blowing him up with a bomb."

"What do you mean, always? You never saw these scrapbooks before."

"Not those." The mother shook her head. "But last year when he and I had the fight, you were going to wire up the television set to a bomb."

"Not the television set," the boy said. "The ignition on his car, so when he stepped on the starter . . ."

"But you didn't do it." The woman's voice was sadly rueful in tone.

"Old lady," the boy said, leaning forward, "this is different. This way, I won't go to jail."

"That's nice."

"That's why a thing like this has to be planned in stages," he said. "So nobody will suspect. You wouldn't want me to go to jail, would you?"

"Oh, no, no, no," the mother said.

"And you going to jail along with me."

"Me?"

"First thing I'd do would be to blame you. For putting me up to it."

"You wouldn't do a thing like that to your mother."

"No?"

"What did I ever do to you?" she said plaintively.

"It takes a genius to figure something like this out," he said easily. "No genius should be in jail."

"No," his mother said. "Of course not."

"It isn't just a matter of a time bomb. It needs know-how —months and months of study and work. Electronics."

"Of course," the mother agreed. "Electrionics."

"From the electronic to the mechanical, but in orderly phases."

"Orderly faces."

"First phase first."

"Second face second."

"Third phase . . ."

The phone rang.

"It'll be for you," the boy said.

"Then I'll answer it," the mother said, and went out into the front hall where the phone was, saying, "I'm coming, I'm coming," as she went.

She was gone a good while. When she came back, her face was dull, and she said, "What time is it?"

"After ten-thirty," the boy said. "What's the matter?"

The mother looked around the room. Her eyes settled on her son as if she was seeing him tonight for the first time.

She said slowly, "What did you do?"

He frowned in bewilderment. "What did I do?"

"That was the paper. The newspaper. On the phone. What did you do?"

"Old lady," he said, "I don't hear your message. What do you . . ."

"*What did you DO?*" she screamed.

I F IT IS true that half the adult population of the United States is interested in news and the other half in sports, then by eleven o'clock, both through news broadcasts and the telecast of the fight in New York, almost everybody in the country must have known about the Everyinch. The public had become privy to information which at such a stage was usually severely restricted and constrained. The wonderful thing about it—if wonderful is the word—was that, as far as practical value was concerned, the public knew just as much as was known by the private officials.

Some of the public knew more, in a way. In Jamaica, New York, the former wife of Mike Trace, pilot of Coastal 214, heard the broadcasts. Her name was Karen—Karen Trace, for she had kept her married name even after the divorce, feeling that it was the right kind of name for a showgirl-model like herself. She long since had given up even a mild claim to the title of actress.

Things generally had not gone well for Karen Trace. "Karen," her agent had told her not long ago, "you're blond, you're stacked, you're not too old. You haven't got a hell of a lot of talent, but who the hell has? What you need to do is jolt yourself—" his hands moved forward expressively—"upon the public consciousness. You follow me?"

"No," Karen had said. "What am I supposed to do?"

"Do something," the agent said. "Have an affair with a professional football player. Make something out of yourself."

"I don't know any professional football players."

"Make it a baseball player, it shouldn't be a total loss."

"Besides," Karen said, and brought her handkerchief out of her purse, "I don't know what you take me for, Stanley."

"What I take you for is not included in the contract," he said. "Think of me as your income tax consultant. We will lie together. I mean, tell lies."

"The only man in my life was my husband," Karen said.

"If you could only sing," Stanley the agent said. "I have a song writer who did a song you could go around singing all the time. It goes—" He began to sing, surprisingly well for a flesh peddler:

> *For him, she was the first of many,*
> *For her, he was the last of few;*
> *And tell me if you know of any*
> *Who ever made that kind of love come true.*
> *For him, she was a mere beginning,*
> *For her he was the last, the end;*
> *Sometimes there's nothing to be won in the*
> *winning—*
> *You wind up with a broken heart to mend,*
> *If you are the first of many, my friend.*

"That's very nice, Stanley," Karen said.

"And you just interchange the pronouns if you want to sing it first person," Stanley said. "For him, *I* was the first of many—for *me*, he was the last of few. You see?"

"I'd like to make a record of that song," Karen said.

"Too bad you can't sing," Stanley said.

The funny thing was, she had heard the song one time since then—sung in a night club where she sat, slothfully attended by an ebullient buyer from Cleveland, only five or six tables away from her former husband. It was the only time since the divorce that she had seen Mike Trace. He was in the company of a tall, good-looking girl, and the girl's name was Emmy. Karen knew this because she had heard Mike call her that; had heard him because she had excused herself and gone toward Mike's table, intending to stop and say something—that something would only have been hello—on the way to the ladies' room. But Mike was deeply in conversation with the other girl, and did not see her; and she had paused only for a fleeting moment, and then continued on her way.

But it was strange that she should hear that song at that time.

She was a mixture, Karen was, and none of the bad things in her deprived her of the right to keep on loving her former husband.

Tonight the mixture bubbled. Things were going very badly indeed with Karen Trace, and now there was the news on the television about Mike's plane.

Karen went to the kitchenette of her apartment and made herself some iced tea. Then, holding the glass in her hand, she went to the telephone and called the number of one of New York's largest newspapers. She told the switchboard girl who answered that she wanted to talk to someone about information she had on the missing airplane, and she was put through to the city desk.

"I just thought you'd like to know," she told the desk man, "that a friend of mine used to be married to the pilot of that plane. Yes, the Coastal plane. She's a model. A good-looking girl. Yes. Her name is Karen Trace. I can give you her telephone number." She read her own phone number to the man at the other end. "What? Yes, I think she's home. If you call right away, I'm sure you'll get her."

THERE WAS rumor and there was puzzlement, and they worked in a strange way to affect a man named Louis Kramer, head of Air Traffic Control for the New York metropolitan area. Kramer—he might have been related to the Kramers whose daughter and son-in-law were aboard Coastal 214; at least the names were spelled the same— was fifty-six years old, a veteran of almost all phases of aviation; tonight he had been at LaGuardia on another mission, but he stayed on to watch fresh developments on Coastal 214.

About eleven o'clock he looked up from the map that had been spread on the desk in the airport manager's office and shook his head. Joe Donaldson, the day tower supervisor at LaGuardia, said, "I don't know. Maybe they find him. Maybe they don't."

"Yup," Kramer said distantly. He was thinking of something else.

"Of course, we assume something stays afloat. There was that plane that just plain blew up in the air crossing Lake Michigan six or seven years ago." Donaldson looked at the other man.

Kramer said slowly, "Joe, there's something here."

"I don't know," Donaldson said. "We've been over it all. We've got everything they've had to report so far."

"No," Kramer said. He was thinking the words a fraction ahead of saying them. "I don't mean the official reports. I mean the fact that the public already knows about it."

"I hear it was a leak they haven't traced yet," Donaldson said. "Marshall Kent of Coastal is fit to be tied. They tell me he's spitting nails."

Kramer shook his head again. "The world is full of people. It's got more people in it than you can shake a stick at. No matter where something happens nowadays, there's somebody there to see it. No real reason for it to hold true all the time, except that it just seems to."

"You're right," Donaldson said. "More or less."

"More, not less," Kramer said. "When those two planes

fell into the Grand Canyon—the most desolate part of the whole country—it turned out three people had seen them fall."

"And?" Donaldson said.

"And the ocean's the same way. Boats, planes, people all over the place."

"Ah, come on," Donaldson said. "There are plenty of crashes nobody ever sees. This time of night—black outside, raining like hell?"

"I'm not worried about people seeing it," Kramer said. He began to pace the floor. "I'm worried about the ones who didn't."

Donaldson looked at him. "What's that mean?"

Kramer stopped pacing. "Look, the whole country is in on this. By now, somebody's had plenty of time to say he saw it happen, or heard it, or something." He tapped the desk with open palm. "There's human nature here. You hear about something exciting, something disastrous, something big, and you identify yourself with it. You picture yourself in a hero's role. You see a light in the sky, you hear a plane, then you find out about this business over the radio and television and if you were five hundred miles from the place, right away you have to tell somebody you were in on it. Maybe you lie like hell. Okay. But . . ."

"But what?" Donaldson said.

Kramer shrugged. "Where are the liars tonight? There hasn't been anybody to say anything."

C. Bertram Ameil, sixty-four years old, might have been the kind of person Kramer had in mind, though he lived a bit north of the probable crash area. Ameil had reacted just as Kramer said the average human would react.

Ameil was positioned for the part. He lived with his wife on Ocracoke Island, just south of Hatteras off Pamlico Sound from the North Carolina coast. It was a lonely existence. Electric lights and the telephone had reached the island, but curiously they had not, even though they could light up the night and sound forth the day, reduced the loneliness.

C. Bertram Ameil was a member of the Ground Observer Corps.

A little while before eleven o'clock, Ameil took his long-powered flashlight and his rain slicker and hat and boots and made ready to go outside.

"Judith," he said to his wife, "where is there a pencil and paper?"

"You're not going out tonight," she said.

"I'm not, hey?"

"There's nothing to see."

"Didn't you hear the radio?"

"That plane," his wife said. "I know. Well, between the sea and the rain, you'd never hear it, and between the clouds and the night you'd never see it, and there's nothing to see or hear anyway because it's crashed long before now, poor souls."

"Same talk I always hear from you," Ameil said, and snorted. "What do you think the Ground Observer Corps is for?"

"Not for catching pneumonia looking for an airplane that's already crashed a long ways from here and if it hadn't you couldn't see it or hear it anyway."

"That's your version," Ameil said. He set the rain hat upon his head.

"You're going out there?" his wife said.

"What do you think?"

"You'll get sick and have to keep your feet in a pan of Epsom salts."

"I'm due to take a tour out there anyway," Ameil said.

"If it wasn't for that radio, you wouldn't have even thought of it," his wife said, "and you know it."

"Now, Mother," Ameil said.

"Don't 'Now, Mother' me." Her eyebrows went up. "When I think that the defense of this country is in the hands of such as you. Suppose you did see something out there tonight. Who would you tell about it?"

"Interceptor Command," Ameil said importantly.

"Ah ha! Interceptor Command!" his wife said. "If I was the phone operator I wouldn't even put you through. How many times have you called them already with your false alarms?"

"I'm doing my duty for my country," Ameil said. "A man's never too old for that. And my motto is, better safe than sorry."

"You already did your duty to your country. The First World War."

"I never got over there."

"No. Your motto was better safe than sorry then too."

"Every man does his duty as he sees it," Ameil said.

"Does that include the boy who shouted 'Wolf'?"

"I tell them what I see."

"They don't seem to believe you."

"That's their privilege."

"Face up to it, Father," she said to him. "Maybe they know better than you."

"I accept their verdict and do my duty none the less," Ameil said.

"Here we go," his wife said. "The speech."

"Government is greater than any individual," Ameil said.

"Government should be no greater than any individual," his wife said.

"I'm not going to listen to this," Ameil said.

"You're a Communist and you always were," Mrs. Ameil said.

"You're an old lady and the only person in the world who could get away with saying that," Ameil said.

"You're an old man and a Communist."

"A person has a duty to serve his government."

"A government has a duty to let a person alone."

"They let me alone. I'm a volunteer, that's what I am."

"You're a Communist, that's what you are. You think anything in the world—pneumonia and all the rest—don't mean a thing. And when the government you're serving comes out and as much as says you're a crazy old man, what do you say? You say the state knows best, that's what you say."

"I happen to be," Ameil said to her, "a member of the Ground Observer Corps—an outfit set up by a capitalist form of government."

"According to Karl Marx you're a Communist."

"According to Thomas Jefferson, you're a crazy old lady."

The man did not know what he was talking about and the woman did not know what she was talking about, which placed them even with most people.

"Senator McCarthy would call you a Communist," the woman said now.

"Senator McCarthy wouldn't know a Communist if he found one under the bed," the man said.

"I suppose that's your final word on the subject," the woman said.

"That's my final word on the subject," Ameil said, and banged out the door.

Within the half hour he was back, the rain glistening on his face. He drew a hand across his eyes, shakingly, and shucked off his coat and said to his wife, "You hear it?"

"Get those boots off'n my clean floor," she said from the wicker chair where she sat beside the radio. "Hear what?"

"If you'd ever get it into your head to turn down the radio, you'd hear something once in a while," Ameil said in a croaking voice. He moved to the radio and turned it off. Then he went inside to the phone. When the operator asked for the number, he said, "Interceptor Command."

"Hold your hats, boys," Mrs. Ameil said from the chair. "Father, will you hang up that phone?"

Ameil shook his head wildly at her, and she saw that his body seemed to be quaking. "Hello," he said. "Hello. Hello?"

"Now, there, you went and got yourself a chill and the shivers," his wife said to him. "You see? You're too *old* to be . . ."

"This is Ameil, Ocracoke," he said into the telephone. "I saw it. Just now." He took a deep breath. "That missing Coastal plane. Flew right over me. Little more than a mile from here—four mile from Ocracoke Center. What? With my flashlight, that's how! What? Of course it's raining. The plane was down underneath the clouds. Couldn't have been no more than five hundred foot off the ground. What? Headed north, that's which way. I could see it, that's how I know. The wing lights? Yes, they were . . ." He stopped, and a strange look came over his face.

His wife was watching him through the doorway from the other room. She shook her head slowly, and there was a small, mirthless smile upon her face.

Ameil said into the telephone, "This plane didn't have any wing lights. This plane didn't have any lights at all."

part three: THE EVERYINCH

THE ENSIGN in the radar room at the Norfolk Naval Base said, "Oh-oh. Get the lieutenant!"

The lieutenant came in and said, "What is it now?"

"Look at that," the ensign said.

The lieutenant looked. He said, "What do you think it is?"

"I think it's that plane, sir."

"The Coastal plane?"

"Yes, sir."

"It can't be."

"It'd be just about plot course."

"How long has that blip been there?"

"Just now."

"But it's in on the screen. How did it get there?"

The ensign swallowed. "It just—appeared."

"What do you mean, it just appeared?"

"It just appeared."

"But that Coastal plane is down."

"Yes, sir. I know, sir."

"There are grave responsibilities here, do you know that?"

Here comes the lecture, the ensign said to himself. *And he doesn't know any more about it than I do.*

"We might have to shoot that plane down," the lieutenant said, thoughtfully. "How many people did they say were on it?"

"Sixteen, sir," the ensign said.

"Expendables," the lieutenant said. "That *is* a blip, isn't it?"

"Yes, sir."

"Put yourself in Soviet shoes for a moment," the lieutenant said. "What would be a perfect way to attack undetected? Shoot down a commercial airliner on a regularly scheduled run over water, then you take that airliner's place. Think, my boy. Use the brains the good Lord gave you."

"Yes, sir, I'm thinking," the ensign said.

"Some clever idea, hey?" the lieutenant said.

"Yes, sir," the ensign said. "But wouldn't we have seen

124

the Russian approaching before he shot our plane down?"

"Don't underestimate the Russians," the lieutenant said.

ONE OF THE phones rang in the office at LaGuardia where Kramer and Donaldson were. Donaldson answered it, and when he hung up he nodded his head, almost in wonder. "Lou," he said, "you were right."

"What's that?" Kramer said.

"You said there was bound to be somebody. That was it."

"What'd they say?"

"Message from the Signal Corps. An Air Force interceptor station heard from one of those civilian ground observers. They say unofficially they hear from him all the time. An old fellow on that island just south of Hatteras."

"Hatteras?" Kramer said, and moved to the map. "That's too far north."

"Not if he's not down, it isn't."

"He saw him?"

Joe Donaldson shrugged. "Play it any way you want. Guy claims the plane flew over him in the rain, headed north, at about five hundred feet."

"When?"

"I don't know," Donaldson said. "They said the guy was nearly a mile away from the phone, but I guess he had a car. Call it maybe fifteen minutes ago, twenty at the outside. Maybe less than that.

"Apparently he's one of those old guys. You know. Know what he said about this one? Said he could see it with his flashlight in the rain and all. So they asked him about the plane's lights."

"And?"

"He said it didn't have any."

"Wow," Kramer said. Another phone rang, and he picked it up and said, "Kramer. Who'd you want to talk to?" He waited for a moment, then said, "That's what it said? All right. Look. Can you get me New York ATC on this phone? Good. Right away. I'll hold on here." He covered the mouthpiece of the receiver with his free hand and said to Donaldson, "Among other things, that report happened to be true."

"What report?"

"The old man."

"*What?*"

"Radar. Virginia Beach. They just picked him up."

"The plane?"

Kramer nodded, and the other phone rang. Donaldson grabbed it and took the newest report. "Radar at Elizabeth City and Beaufort confirming," he said across the room to Kramer. "Unidentified aircraft on their screens. Compass course just east of due north."

Kramer nodded again. He was talking into his phone now: ". . . and make sure all reports are phoned into this office. Meanwhile, get me Washington on the phone . . ."

Donaldson had hung up his phone, but now it rang again, and again he picked it up. He said, "What? Yes, Colonel. Yes, we just heard about it. What's that? Wait a minute." In turn he covered the mouthpiece of his phone and said to Kramer, "Hey, Lou. The military."

"What do they want?" Kramer said.

"He wants to know if this is a definite identification, commercial aircraft."

"No more definite," Kramer said, "except that who else would it be?"

"That's what the colonel wants to know."

"Give me that," Kramer said, and took the phone. "Colonel, this is Kramer, New York . . . oh, George. How you feel? Yuh, we've got it. Just came in here. What? Oh, wait a minute, George, hold on for a second. You have an estimated speed on the aircraft?" He nodded into the phone. "Then it's got to be propeller-driven. It's on course for our plane, and there are no other commercial or civilian craft flight-planned in the area. All right, put it this way. There are others, but they're all accounted for. What do you mean, potential enemy? You think this is Pearl Harbor? One lousy propeller-driven . . . I know, George. I know it only takes one. Ah, now, what is this crazy talk? What enemy is going to fly a propeller plane north up the Atlantic Coast in a rainstorm and where did he start from to begin with? Miami?" He sighed. "And what are you going to do about it? You military give me a swift pain. You spend millions of dollars figuring out how to hit something and nobody ever spends a quarter figuring out how to avoid getting hit. You've got jets and missiles that can shoot down my plane in four seconds flat, but you haven't got a goddam thing that can go up there and identify him. You've got jets on the ready, but they go too fast and my guy's got no lights. They'd never even see him. What? How the hell do I know what he's going to do next? You think you've got troubles? Mine are just beginning!"

THUS THE FIRST circle had come full. What Ed Benson had guessed at, back in ATC in Jacksonville when Coastal 214 first failed to report, was, all succeeding rumor and guesswork to the contrary, simply the truth. It had, as

127

Benson had remembered, happened just that way to a commercial Boston–New York flight early in 1956. Now it had happened to the Everyinch.

The radio and electrical systems were out.

Actually, it was one system that had shorted out. It had shorted by accident, and not through the doing of any person, least of all Herman Jonas' imaginative stepson in Miami, who had not the opportunity, the material, or probably, for that matter, the guts, to put his long-standing visionary plan of sabotage into action. The boy had not got near the plane.

There are in all modern aircraft two wholly independent electrical systems. In the case of the Boston–New York flight, just as in the case of the Everyinch now, there was no loss of power. The engines, on one electrical system, continued to run perfectly, with the magnetos continuing to supply the necessary power for firing the spark plugs. Hydraulic mechanical equipment, such as rudder, flaps, landing gear, even windshield wipers, continued to operate normally.

But the second electrical system, governing the fuselage, lights, radios, and all components independent of the engines, remains wholly separate. It is generated by alternators mounted on the engines themselves, but these power plants have no tie-in with the electrical system required by the engines—that is, the magnetos. And in the Boston–New York flight, just as now in Coastal 214, these generators on the engines, which were independently supplying the airplane's second electrical system with their power, had shorted and gone dead, thus killing the lights, radio, intercom, and instruments, but not affecting the plane's power plants in the slightest.

The crew of the Everyinch knew this and knew exactly

what had happened, though it was still a matter of guess-work on the ground. Mike Trace, the pilot, had decided not to try to turn back to Miami, even though the trouble had happened just a little time after take-off. He was not too concerned about other traffic in the sky—radar would see him turn around; rather, he was concerned about it, but more concerned about the weather. Trying to find his way back in rain and clouds, without instruments, would be one of the more hazardous courses open to him.

All but two of his major instruments were out. The two still functioning were of vital importance, but neither could be relied upon for certain accuracy in the absence of other corroborating instruments and information.

The magnetic compass was one of these instruments—true only as its original setting was true, becoming a little less true all the time as the plane headed northward, coming closer all the time to the pole. The pressure altimeter was the other, operating as a barometer. But this gave a correct reading only if you knew from other information, including a radio altimeter, what the sea level barometric pressure was at the point you were passing over. If you knew what sea level pressure was, your barometric altimeter told you your height above sea level. Mike Trace did not know what sea level pressure was.

What had he done? He had decided, apparently, to trust his operating altimeter to a certain point, to come down at least a certain distance in an effort to see where he was. In coming down, he had at last reached the point where the Everyinch literally disappeared from radar screens—he was under the lip of radar scansion, having become the "low-flying aircraft" that the Ground Observer Corps was or-ganized for the purpose of spotting.

Now he had made landfall just south of Hatteras, and his

next move would be a matter of careful choice. Unless he had some way of knowing for certain that those on the ground knew exactly who and where he was, an attempted landing at some fairly convenient airport would be risky—assuming that he could spot the airport and had in the flight cabin enough light from flashlights to read his airport recognition charts. A landing in the water would be at least equally hazardous. If he continued to fly below the ceiling in an effort to assure his own knowledge of his position, he ran other risks. At least if he regained sufficient altitude to assume he could be seen again on radar, then other planes would be warned out of his path, and if anything else went wrong, if he had to come down in the ocean, the groundlings would have a recent idea of where he was. Besides, if anything did go wrong—an engine cutting out, for instance—then the more altitude he had, the better his chance of dealing with such emergency in flight.

All this had been the pilot's thinking, but now, at last, it began to coincide with the thinking of those on the ground. Now they began to assume certain things. From the fact that he had been spotted by a ground observer while underneath the radar, then seen again on the screens, they knew he had climbed once more. They assumed that he would not have done this unless he had succeeded in the purpose which caused him to come down to begin with—finding out where he was. He must have recognized the lights of Ocracoke and Hatteras and the mainland to the left.

And if he recognized where he was, then he must know something else. His magnetic compass was serving him well, because Ocracoke and Hatteras were almost directly on course for tonight's mapped plan for Coastal 214.

This, for the time being, was where the ground assumptions left off. But another one was beginning to suggest itself. It was strange, fearsome in its way, and difficult to contemplate, but it had to be thought about.

Coastal 214, if it continued on its present course, would be entering the area of the most heavily traveled air in the world—without lights, without radio, without the slightest illumination from a rain-clogged sky. In this respect, this was the most hazardous thing the pilot could do.

Under the circumstances, it was also, with equal certainty, the least hazardous. The safest thing the pilot could do, knowing where he was, would be to go where he was expected to go:

LaGuardia.

It was not through Mike Trace's brother Willard that the first announcement of the new development leaked this time to the public. On the other hand, Willard's services were not needed this time, either. Marshall Kent, vice-president of Coastal Airlines, who had so opposed the idea of making earlier information public, now saw to it personally that the wire services were notified immediately. The news that the plane was *not* down had to be made public as soon as possible, though it did not remove Kent's bitterness that the earlier bulletins had got out. (What was it he had told Willard Trace over the phone at the first indication of trouble? "I don't want the papers hearing about it . . . if he's up there and on course then there's nothing seriously wrong." And events to this moment now proved him right. Not that his airline was out of the woods by any means. Not that it was yet known for certain, on the ground, what exactly had gone wrong with this craft, or exactly when, or how, or why; not that the most perilous part of the journey did not still lie ahead. Not even that under any conditions the story would not have had to come out later anyway.) But while there was life, there was hope, and there was life now and an aircraft in flight, where before the radio and television had been proclaiming an ocean crash.

So Kent saw to it the news agencies were notified.

Then he prepared to leave the home of Felix Allerdyce to go out to LaGuardia.

Allerdyce said to him, "Well, I'm happy for you."

"Why?" Kent said.

"Well," Allerdyce said, "your plane hasn't crashed."

"Not yet, it hasn't," Kent said. "When I think of all those fish in cargo and that new contract and all those restaurants."

"It certainly makes you stop and think, doesn't it?" Allerdyce said fecklessly. "Well, I certainly hope everything comes all right. For my sake as well as yours."

"Your sake?" Kent said, and Allerdyce saw that he had said the wrong thing.

"I mean," said Allerdyce, "I was looking forward to some of those fish. I'm a great fan of Florida sea food."

"I just want to get that plane landed," Kent said. "That's all I want."

"Well, they have a pretty good idea of his whereabouts now," Allerdyce said. "He can come down any time now. Belly-land in the water, launch his rafts, and everybody'll be saved." He thought for a moment, then brightened. "Chances are they'll get that cargo off too. A little water never hurt a fish."

"That's nice," Kent said to him. "The plane comes down in the water, hey?"

"It's the practical thing to do, I'd say," Allerdyce said. "Maneuver in close to shore where he can be seen. Those pilots know their business. He can land her in the water, they'll have boats out there to take everybody off in less than ten minutes, and meanwhile he won't be jockeying his way through all those other planes in the sky looking for an airport. Chesapeake Bay, now. That'd be a good place to . . ."

Kent was looking at him. "If that son-of-a-bitch of a pilot has that on his mind, I'll kill him. I'll kill him with my own hands."

"Why?" Allderdyce said. "What's the matter? Isn't it safest to . . ."

"I lose an airplane that way, that's what's the matter," Kent said. "Did that ever occur to that stupid head of yours?"

"Well," Allerdyce said thickly, "things like that are insured, aren't they? Just like anything else?"

"Yes, it's insured," Kent said. "And meanwhile, where do I get another airplane? You got an answer for that one too?"

"I wonder," Allerdyce said aloud, musingly. He had given up all hope of securing the Coastal advertising account by now. "Suppose the Army or somebody had some trigger-happy scarecrow somewhere who decided that thing on radar wasn't your plane, but an enemy plane instead. It might still happen, for all they tell you it won't."

Kent stared at him.

"Suppose the Army went up and shot it down," Allerdyce said. "Would your insurance policy pay off?"

"Oh, my God," Kent said, and headed for the door.

"Good night, Marshall," Allerdyce called after him. "The pleasure was mine."

And he turned and went over to the television set and switched it on, and the first thing he got was his headache commercial.

F ROM A NEWS agency's standpoint, the story now was more exciting than ever.

Neither Global Press nor any other news organization knew all of the data that went into it. They did not grasp the significance of the simple fact that the plane, when spotted, was on course. They did not know that auxiliary equipment, such as rudder and wheels, was in working order. Some of these things, they could not have been expected to know. Others they could have deduced with a little logic. If the plane had gone down, then gone up again, it at least made sense that whatever it was that made an airplane go up and down was operating properly.

But aside from the technicalities, they knew a story when they saw it, and rarely had they seen one like this.

The new lead from the typewriter of Harry Timmons at GPA said what all the news services were saying now:

BULLETIN NEW LEAD ALL PLANE

A FOUR-ENGINE COASTAL AIRLINES PLANE WITH SIXTEEN PERSONS ABOARD IS FLYING NORTH ALONG THE HEAVILY TRAVELED AIRWAYS OFF THE ATLANTIC COAST TONIGHT—WITHOUT LIGHTS, WITHOUT IN-STRUMENTS, WITHOUT RADIO.

FEARED EARLIER TO HAVE CRASHED IN THE RAIN-TOSSED SEAS, THE PLANE IS NOW VISIBLE ONCE MORE,

THOUGH ONLY ON RADAR. COASTAL AIRLINES SAYS THERE IS NO DOUBT THIS IS THE SAME PLANE THAT FAILED TO MAKE A SCHEDULED 8:04 RADIO CONTACT SHORTLY AFTER TAKING OFF NONSTOP, MIAMI TO NEW YORK, THEN LATER WAS LOST FOR A TIME FROM RADAR CONTACT TOO.

APPARENTLY THE PLANE, WHICH HAS FOUR CHILDREN AMONG ITS TWELVE PASSENGERS, DESCENDED FOR A TIME UNDERNEATH THE EFFECTIVE SWEEP OF CIRCULATING RADAR CONES ON THE EARTH AS THE PILOT, MICHAEL TRACE OF ROSLYN HEIGHTS, N. Y., SOUGHT TO GET UNDERNEATH THE CLOUDS TO FIND OUT WHERE HE WAS. IN SO DOING, HE WAS SPOTTED, THE AIRLINE SAID, BY A LONELY MEMBER OF THE GROUND OBSERVER CORPS, AT HIS POST IN THE DRIVING RAIN ON CAPE HATTERAS.

THE UNSUNG HERO WHO FLASHED NEWS OF THE PLANE'S WHEREABOUTS WAS IDENTIFIED AS C. B. AMEIL, 64, OCRACOKE ISLAND, N. CAR. SIGNAL CORPS AUTHORITIES SAID AMEIL WAS ONE OF THE FIRST AMERICANS TO VOLUNTEER FOR THE GROUND OBSERVER CORPS WHEN IT WAS FIRST ESTABLISHED. A MILITARY OFFICIAL SAID AMEIL HAD RELAYED "SEVERAL TIPS" IN THE PAST, BUT NONE SO VALUABLE AS TONIGHT'S.

WHAT THE FATE OF THE PLANE WILL BE NOW IS A QUESTION THAT HAS OFFICIALS, RELATIVES AND FRIENDS OF THOSE ABOARD, AND, INDEED, THE ENTIRE NATION, FRANTICALLY GUESSING . . . AND HOPING.

ABOARD THE PLANE ARE THE WIFE AND CHILD OF TONIGHT'S SENSATIONAL BOXING STAR ALBIE WEBBER, WHO . . .

Timmons couldn't get Webber any higher than that this time around, but nobody took him to task for it. Max Wild, the general manager of GPA, did come out of his office to raise a little discreet hell about the quality of the lead.

"You can make it more exciting than that," he told the rewrite man.

"Come on, Max," Timmons said. "Nobody has to manufacture excitement for this one. It's built in, I'd say."

"Let me at the typewriter for a minute," Wild said. He sat down, thought for a minute, then wrote:

> first new lead
> a giant ghost in the sky—a blacked-out four-engine coastal airlines plane flying without lights, instruments or radio—tonight is groping a desperate northward path

"No, wait a minute," Wild said, and tried the last line again:

> tonight is groping blindly northward through black rain clouds over the mid-atlantic seaboard, carrying twelve passengers, four of them children, and a crew of four toward an unknown fate.

"What do you think?" Wild said now.

"I like mine better," Timmons said.

"I don't."

"You used the word 'black' twice—'blacked-out' and 'black rain clouds.' "

"Hell, is that all that's wrong with it?"

"It needs work," Timmons said, but he was on the defensive. The "ghost in the sky" and the "groping blindly" were good. "And you don't have that element of heavy traffic that I had in my lead."

Shortly, the new version was going out over the wires:

BULLETIN OPTIONAL LEAD PLANE

A GIANT GHOST IN THE SKY—A BLACKED-OUT FOUR-ENGINE COASTAL AIRLINES PLANE FLYING WITHOUT RADIO, INSTRUMENTS, OR LIGHTS—TO- NIGHT IS GROPING BLINDLY THROUGH THE MURK OVER THE ATLANTIC SEABOARD WITH THE FATE OF ITS OWN 16 OCCUPANTS—AND THAT OF THOSE ABOARD COUNTLESS OTHER PLANES IN THE HEAVILY TRAVELED SEABOARD VICINITY—A FEARSOME QUES- TION.

For all the nicety of phrasing, Harry Timmons liked his own story better. It was simpler. Besides, Max Wild him- self had formulated a rule at GPA—no lead sentence should exceed 30 words in length. This one, which Wild had both suggested and approved, had 56 words, count 'em.

LIKE THE BALANCE valve in a water line, Ben Gammon now was getting the news from the place where earlier he had been feeding it. One of the night men in the newsroom had phoned him the new bulletin.

"He's still in the sky," Ben said to Emmy, hanging up the phone. "I'm going to make myself a drink whether you like it or not."

"He's alive?" Emmy said. "He's safe?"

"He's alive," Ben said, "and a lot safer than he's been up to now; far as we could tell, anyway." He went over and put his hands on her shoulders, and it was in itself a closer and more meaningful touch than the two of them had had at any time before when they were together. Ironically, it came not only coincident to, but because of, the news that Mike was safe.

Safe up to this point, at least. Gammon told her what the situation was, exactly as he had heard it from his office.

Then she said, "What will happen now?"

"That," Gammon said, "nobody knows. But I'd say his chances were awful good."

She smiled and nodded her head. "Make me a drink, too. Ben?"

"Mmhmm?" he said, moving toward the kitchen.

"Make it a stiff one."

"I didn't know you knew the difference."

"I don't."

"But this is an occasion," he said. He stopped and thought for a moment. "What was that name you called me before?"

"You? I? A name?"

"You look pretty when you're bewildered," Ben said, and recrossed the room, and, without warning and without reason that he could think of, kissed Emmy first on the tip of the nose and then on the mouth, at once artfully and artlessly, and turned once more and went back to the kitchen. Neither of them, at this moment, could fight down the exhilaration and the feeling that now, no matter what, Mike Trace and the Everyinch would be safe.

"The poet," Ben said. "The one I knew the dates for."

"Oh," she said from the living room. "Swinburne. Algernon Charles."

"That's right," Ben said. "1837–1909."

"I'm going to turn up the television," she called.

138

"There might be some news," Gammon said. "Maybe from AP or somebody. Let's see what the oppositions are saying."

Emmy tried a few different stations, and by the time Gammon was back in the living room with the drinks she had found one in mid-broadcast of a bulletin about the plane.

". . . heroic pilot," the announcer was saying, "refused to turn back to Miami even though the trouble was discovered as early as it was, so as not to run the chance of colliding with another aircraft in the clouds over busy Miami Airport. Meanwhile, the . . ."

They listened to it all. When the announcer was through, Gammon said to Emmy, "Here's your drink."

"Stiff one?" She took the glass.

"Whopper."

"Good. Here's to—to what?"

"Mike. Your flyboy."

"The whole plane too," Emmy said. "The rest of the crew. The passengers."

"The cargo of barking dogs and rare jewels," Gammon said. "No. Just to Mike. He's a hero."

"A hero?" Emmy said.

"The television just said so."

"That's right," Emmy said. "It did, didn't it? Because he didn't turn back to Miami. So he wouldn't hit another plane."

"Righto," Gammon said. He did not wait for the toast, but drank deeply.

"But he's not a hero," Emmy said. "Not for that."

"No?"

"No. If he was going to hit another plane, that means

139

his own plane would be hit too. So he must have done it as much for his own sake as anybody else's."

"Well, that's one stinking way of looking at it," Gammon said. "If you don't mind my saying so."

"I don't mind your saying so," Emmy said. "And besides, it would seem to me if his object is to avoid doing damage to other planes, then the longer he stays up in the air the more planes he has a chance of hitting."

"Let me ask you something," Gammon said to her. "You for this guy or against him?"

"Oh, I'm for him, I'm for him," Emmy said. "But he's doing his job. It isn't heroism. Is it?"

"I rather think in a way it is," Gammon said. "I don't know why I'm saying this, but that's what I think."

"It's hard to think of Mike in any kind of trouble," Emmy said. "I'm sorry." She paused. "This drink *is* strong."

"Ah, the hell with it," Gammon said. "Give it back and I'll make you a weak one. A Rhine wine and seltzer."

"No," Emmy said, and maneuvered her glass away from his hand and shook her head. "You don't," she said, solemnly and clearly, "love a man because he's a hero or he's not a hero. You love him because you love him, not because of something they have to say about him on television."

"Because he's just your Bill," Gammon said.

"Shut up," she said to him.

"Oh, no," he said. "Don't say shut up. Just when I remembered poetry by Swinburne, you tell me shut up."

"Quote poetry by Swinburne, then," she said. "But be quiet about everything else."

"Ah," he said archly, "and suppose the poetry also has to do with everything else? With arch connotations." He waved his glass. "Businesses between the lines."

140

"You sound like you know the whole poem."

"I don't. Whisky is not, with me, an aphrodisiac or particularly even a stimulant. What it does is joggle useless flotsam and jetsam from my memory."

"The mobile F and J," Emmy said.

"Exactly," Gammon said, and grinned; inwardly, the fact that she should remember about the mobile F and J brought to him, ridiculously, a remarkable feeling of delight.

"I have some Swinburne in a book," Emmy said. "On that shelf over there somewhere." She settled herself on the couch. "Go find it and then come here and sit next to me, and read me the whole poem."

"Including the title?"

"Including the title."

"Then I'd better do it standing up." He went and found the book on the shelf; looked through it and found what he was looking for.

"The title," he said, "is 'At Parting.'"

" 'At Parting'?"

"Yes. You know. Parting. Leave-taking. Going away."

"Am I supposed to read something between those lines?"

"It's only one line so far. You have to have more than one line in order to read between."

"Ah," she said. "Dialectic."

"That's what the girl said to Sergeant Warden in *From Here to Eternity*," Gammon said. "From listening to the rest of their conversation, you wouldn't dream either one of them knew what 'dialectic' meant."

"Do you?"

"No. Do you?"

"I'm waiting for the poem," Emmy said.

"All right," he said. His voice became louder. "All right."
Then he read the poem:

> For a day and a night Love sang to us, played
>   with us,
>   Folded us round from the dark and the light;
> And our hearts were fulfilled of the music he
>   made with us,
> Made with our hearts and our lips while he stayed
>   with us,
>   Stayed in mid passage his pinions from flight
>   For a day and a night.
>
> From his foes that kept watch with his wings had
>   he hidden us,
>   Covered us close from the eyes that would
>   smite,
> From the feet that had tracked and the tongues
>   that had chidden us
> Sheltering in shade of the myrtles forbidden us
>   Spirit and flesh growing one with delight
>   For a day and a night.
>
> But his wings will not rest and his feet will not
>   stay for us:
>   Morning is here in the joy of its might;
> With his breath has he sweetened a night and a
>   day for us:
> Now let him pass, and the myrtles make way
>   for us;
>   Love can but last in us here at his height
>   For a day and a night.

After he had finished, neither of them said anything for
a time. Finally, Emmy said, "You mean the part about
the wings."

"Not necessarily," he said.

"Necessarily," she said. "What was that about 'not rest'?"

Gammon consulted the book. " 'His wings will not rest and his feet will not stay for us.' "

"I suppose 'us' is you and me," Emmy said, "and the 'wings' are Mike's."

"Drink up your drink," Ben Gammon said to her.

"You know everything, don't you?" she said.

"For a long time I thought I knew everything."

"You found out you didn't?"

"I found out I didn't."

"Did it make any difference?"

"No."

"Not knowing or realizing you didn't know?"

"Both. Neither."

"Oh. The only things you didn't know turned out to be things that didn't matter. Insignificant little nothings."

"No. It was just that whether I knew everything or didn't know everything, it didn't make much difference one way or the other. Who was I going to tell?"

"I don't know," Emmy said. "I'm not sure I follow this. Are you making sense?"

"Maybe. Mike Trace would know. There's a fella makes sense."

EDWARD, the night copy boy at Global Press in New York, came up to Harry Timmons' desk and said, "There's a man outside."

"I'm busy, Edward," Timmons said. "Go obscenity thyself."

"Inside of two years I'm going to be a Rutgers graduate,"

Edward said. "Then you won't talk to me like that any more."

"Inside of two years you might also be the editor-in-chief of Global Press, the way they promote people around here," Timmons said, "and then I won't talk to you like that any more either. But in the meantime, do me a particular favor and go obscenity thyself."

"There's a man outside and he's crying," Edward said.

"He's what?"

"He's crying."

Harry Timmons passed a hand in front of his face. "I don't know what you have to do to make a simple living around here. Who does he want to see?"

"Somebody about the plane."

"What's he doing again?"

"He's crying," Edward said.

"You better send him in here," Timmons said, and Edward went out into the waiting room by the elevators and came back with a little man who had a gray suit and a mustache. The little man had indeed been crying. His eyes were circled with red, and when he spoke his lower lip quivered; but his voice was controlled enough.

"I was in a bar in the neighborhood," he said. "I just heard about it. They told me you'd know up here." He looked pleadingly at Timmons. "Is she on it?"

Timmons said gently, "Who?"

"My wife," the man said.

"Do you want to sit down?" Timmons said. "Edward, why don't you bring this man a glass of water?"

"That would be wonderful, thank you," the little man said. He took out a handkerchief and blew his nose loudly. "I'm sorry I'm making a spectacle."

Timmons smiled a soft smile. "We have every reason to hope for the plane."

"You're sure it didn't crash?"

"That's right."

"They told me downstairs they weren't sure."

"No," Timmons said. He reached for the copy spike. "I can show you the latest bul . . ." He stopped. It occurred to him that the cold, bare-faced news copy, especially as it had been doctored by Max Wild, was not the nicest thing in the world to show the husband of one of the passengers. Timmons realized, even in thinking this, that this same copy was being read over radio and television the nation over; but still, here in this personal atmosphere, it seemed deeply wrong. Then another thought came to him, and he said, "First, you haven't even told me your name."

The other man stared at him for a moment. Then, in comprehension, he took out his wallet and slowly extracted one of his printed cards. He seemed to have immense patience, acting as one might after definite news of a death.

The card said:

K. L. SHERMAN

Human Hair Goods

FLATIRON BUILDING   NEW YORK

Reading the card, Harry Timmons' eyes grew large, and it took an immense fealty to decorum to keep him from asking outright what human hair goods were. Instead, he said, "Well, let me see. Was your wife supposed to be flying back from Miami tonight?"

"I think so," the little man named Sherman said.

"You think so?"

"Yes," Sherman said, and now he began to cry openly. His shoulders shook, and around the newsroom other GPA men looked up from their desks to see what was happening.

"Well, let's check the list," Timmons said, and went down the list with his finger. He said, "Uh-huh. Mrs. K. L. Sherman, New York City?"

"That's Dorothy," the man said, and buried his head in his hands.

Harry Timmons looked around for a moment. Edward, the copy boy, was there with a paper cup filled with water. "Edward," Timmons said to him, "let's you and I take Mr. Sherman here into Mr. Wild's office. He can lie down and rest."

"I didn't know Mr. Wild had a couch," Edward said.

"Edward," Timmons said to him."

"Well, I've never been inside Mr. Wild's office," Edward said. "The closest I ever got was the girl outside who . . ."

"Edward," Timmons said to him. Then, remembering, he bent over the little man and said, "Let's go inside where we can get you something, Mr. Sherman. The last reports we have are that the plane is all right. We can keep you up to the minute with all the news."

"Dorothy," K. L. Sherman said. "Dorothy." He sobbed helplessly as Timmons took his arm and led him toward Max Wild's inner office.

"Edward," Timmons said, "go ahead and tell Mr. Wild we're coming."

Edward swallowed and went ahead, and Max Wild was waiting at the door of his office when Timmons got there with the bereft K. L. Sherman. Wild was the kind of man who reacted and adapted most quickly, and he was ready to help guide Mr. Sherman to the couch inside.

"This is Mr. Sherman," Harry Timmons said. "This is his card." He gave the card to Wild, and Wild looked at it and then looked at Timmons. "His wife is on the plane," Timmons said. (Nobody paid attention to how easily and universally Coastal 214 had become by now merely The Plane.) "He heard about it and came up here for news."

"Well, of course, Mr. Sherman," Max Wild said. "Your wife's going to be all right. May I get you something to drink? Black Label? Neat?"

"Dorothy," K. L. Sherman mumbled brokenly.

"Yes, indeed," Wild said smoothly. "Everything's going to be just fine, Mr. Sherman. Human hair goods, hey? Must be fascinating, Mr. Sherman, fascinating. I'm Max Wild, the general manager of Global Press Association . . ."

Harry Timmons and Edward, the copy boy, closed the door on their way out.

"Mr. Timmons?" Edward said.

"What is it, Edward?" Timmons said. Mentally, he noted the time and calculated it would take Max Wild no more than twenty minutes to get a human interest story (a human hair interest story?) under the by-line of K. L. Sherman. It would make a fine sidebar to the main plane story for the GPA wires.

"Some time when you have a minute, Mr. Timmons," Edward the copy boy said, "I would like you to explain something to me."

"Really?" Timmons said, moving swiftly back toward his desk in the newsroom with Edward trotting at his shoulder. "What's that, Edward?"

"Everybody says you know about money," Edward said.

"That's because I was Guild treasurer for a year one time," Timmons said. "Think nothing of it." He noticed that in his absence, somebody else had handled a news box about the father of one of the other occupants of Coastal 214. It was a cute item. William Goldstone, father of Marvin Goldstone who was the flight engineer on the Everyinch, had just now landed at LaGuardia on a flight from Kansas City. Goldstone the elder, the man who always knew that flying was safe, did not hear about the trouble with Coastal 214 till he stepped off the plane at the end of his journey.

Edward the copy boy said to Timmons now, "I would like you to explain the monetary system to me."

"You would?" Timmons said.

"Yes," Edward said. "I mean, there are things I don't understand."

"I wouldn't have believed it of you, Edward," Timmons said. "What don't you understand?"

"Well, for example," Edward said, "if the Government owes me five hundred dollars for something I did for them on contract or something, they send me a check for five hundred dollars. Then let's say I borrowed five hundred from you. I endorse the Government's check over to you. Then let's say you owe five hundred in Federal income tax. You endorse the check over to the Government. So everybody got paid and nobody spent a quarter. How does that happen?"

"Why do you ask me?" Timmons said. "What the hell are you going to Rutgers for?"

148

Now it was past midnight, and radar watched the Everyinch and marveled that the plane deviated not at all from course (though he could be under the clouds by now—the ceiling ranged up to 2,000). Coastal 214 was just off the shoreline, fifty miles south of Atlantic City, New Jersey, and in New York, ATC watched and waited. For the three metropolitan airports—Newark, LaGuardia, Idlewild—flight plans showed a total of forty-seven commercial aircraft scheduled to arrive in the half-hour period between 12:55 A.M. and 1:25 A.M.—the spread that now seemed inevitable for the arrival of Coastal 214 itself (assuming the pilot did not decide to land at some other field en route).

Weather had steadied all along the coast now, though exact ceilings at given points were changing from minute to minute. In New York it was still over 1,000, more than it had been at Hatteras when Coastal 214 had come down to get under the clouds off the Carolinas. Apparently, the Everyinch had come down several times since, just enough to get under the clouds and give the pilot a visual fix—that would account for his steady course; also for the fact that he was by now as far behind schedule as he was.

Kramer and Donaldson, in the tower now at LaGuardia, talked about it.

"He'd better come down pretty soon," Kramer said.

"Maybe he is," Donaldson said. "Somebody on that plane must have a wrist watch."

"That's true," Kramer said.

"If he recognized Hatteras he'd know how long it took him to get there from Miami," Donaldson said. "He figures in his time lost descending and going back up again, keeps his speed as constant as he can without knowing if the wind shifts or not. That way he ought to be able to figure New York."

"He's got to be up in clouds now," Kramer said.

"Well," Donaldson said, "what can we do?"

"Everything possible," Kramer said. "Let's get it straight again. Searchlights?"

"Every damn searchlight from Cape May north," Donaldson said crisply. "Including a dozen ships at sea that we know of. Of course, some of them don't have searchlight power enough to help a hell of a lot, but you never can tell."

"Plane arrivals?"

"Every airport, commercial and military, from Philadelphia north under instructions," Donaldson said. "Land all incoming planes. Take-offs as scheduled but not at the expense of any incoming aircraft even on the fringe of tower control."

"Well, we don't have to do *that*," Kramer said.

"It won't make that much difference, according to the traffic we'll be having," Donaldson said. "And besides, towers can act at their own discretion up to the time we put them on final alert."

"I think he's going to be all right," Kramer said. "If you want the truth of it."

Donaldson looked at him. "You're sure he's coming here?"

"No," Kramer said. "No, I'm not. But I'm less sure of anything else. All I know is, this is where he's supposed to come."

"Assuming he comes into New York at all," Donaldson said, "it seems to me there are a number of safer things he could do."

"Such as?"

"Land at Floyd Bennett or Idlewild—give him that much less traffic to cut through. Ditch in the ocean alongside one of the beaches—keep him away from airport traffic completely and still give him shallow water and a heavily populated beach line, so he'll be sure to be noticed."

"Yes and no," Kramer said. "For that matter, he could land at Atlantic City, but he obviously isn't going to. Remember, this pilot hasn't come into any New York airport except LaGuardia in four years. He knows this field. He'd have to check charts on any other and even then he wouldn't have the feel of it. Go down in the water—I don't know. He's got no landing lights. It's still raining pretty tough out there, regardless of the ceiling. To be that close to a dozen airports and put his plane in the water, at that much more risk to his passengers and cargo and at God knows what kind of loss to the plane itself he might figure we'd think he was crazy instead of smart, and who knows what he thinks his bosses might think. That guy Kent at Coastal is a maniac."

"But you just said it was raining," Donaldson said. "Suppose he comes straight into LaGuardia. Ceiling or no ceiling, as you say, he's supposed to come in on instrument and radio in the rain. Sure, once he's got the field in view, that's one thing. But what about before that? Where's his visual fix coming in? Coney Island? Is Coney lit up in the rain? Hell, no. Night ball game at Ebbets Field? Not in the rain."

"Look," Kramer said to him, "you see New York from the sky at night and you're an airline pilot, brother, you know where you are. Rain or no rain."

"Well," Donaldson said, "are we arguing or are we trying

to think with the pilot? A tired pilot. Don't forget that. Been through five hours of the damnedest strain you can imagine, and the most deadly part of it is coming up now. *This* is where he can crash his plane the easiest. *This* is where he's got a ten times greater chance of hitting another plane in the air."

"Maybe he's tired," Kramer said.

"You don't think he is?"

Kramer shrugged. "There are all kinds of theories about pilot fatigue. One of them has to do with hypnosis—the same kind you get driving your car hour after hour along a superhighway. And what's the greatest inducement to that hypnosis?"

"The hum of the engines," Donaldson said. "He's got that."

"I don't know," Kramer said. "The thing that bothered me most when I was flying wasn't the noise. It was the view."

"The view?"

"I don't mean the view from the plane. I mean the view when you can't see out. That lighted instrument panel. Dial after dial. Sitting there. The lights on each instrument. More than a hundred dials. Each one individually lit. The dials never seeming to move, any of them. Just sitting there."

"Well, he hasn't got any dials lit up," Donaldson said. "That's for sure."

"Best we can do is wait and see," Kramer said, and gazed out the window into the rain. The window commanded a full-circle view, and now, looking southeast, away from the field and toward the approach roads and parking lots at the airport and the Grand Central Parkway beyond, Kramer frowned and stared. "Joe," he said, "what are all those lights?"

Donaldson came and looked out the window. "My God," he said.

"They can't be automobiles," Kramer said.

"They are automobiles," Donaldson said. His tone was one of complete disbelief. "Thousands of them."

THE PORT AUTHORITY cops at the Triborough Bridge had reported it first. At this time of night there were only two lanes open at the Manhattan entrance, two others at the Bronx.

It was like the night of the locust.

Seemingly in one fell swoop, the traffic had piled up upon them, reaching endlessly. And the bridge to Queens became black with midnight traffic pouring in that direction.

New York police were quick to sense what it was. Thousands upon thousands were headed for LaGuardia Field. They did not know that was where Coastal 214 was going to land. They knew only that that was where Coastal 214 was supposed to land. They were operating from there on pure instinct—the instinct of a mob that is not itself in danger: at many times the most certain instinct of all.

In that growing crush, only one automobile had any real business being there. It was a 1939 Chevrolet, and in it were seven persons, all named Diaz, from East Harlem. They had heard the radio. One reporter had found them—a reporter from a New York paper which had been tipped by one of their neighbors—but they had not let him in the flat they occupied; had chased him away with threats and imprecations. Their relative, Rafael Diaz, and his wife and three of their children, all from Puerto Rico, were aboard that plane. Something told them they must go to LaGuardia. They went the best way they knew how. It had not occurred to them that the police or the newspapers or the airline would help them. To the police they were criminals, to the papers they were statistics on delinquency and crime, to the airlines they were no more than paying cattle. This was their thinking.

They were there in the creeping, horn-blowing, Roman holiday midnight traffic on the Triborough Bridge. Stuck there.

BUT THE DIAZES were at least accounted for, and now, with Coastal 214 watched on radar as it passed Atlantic City, the entire passenger list was accounted for, and the crew as well, as far as kinfolk on the ground were concerned. The officials or the airline or the press had, one way and another, made contact with those closest to the four members of the crew and the passengers—the wife and child of the fighter Albie Webber; the newlyweds, Mr. and Mrs. James Laurie; Herman Jonas, the man from Miami; the Diaz family; and Mrs. K. L. Sherman, wife of the man in human hair goods.

The entire list? Not quite.

There was one name on the passenger list that had no accompanying address.

In the city rooms of newspapers around the country, and in other places too, the question seemed most appropriate.

The mishap that had befallen Coastal 214 was nothing if not mysterious.

An added touch of mystery would hardly be out of place.

The unknown extra passenger.

Who was John Black?

THE PHONE rang in Emmy Verdon's apartment, and it was Ben Gammon's office, calling him.

"Ben?" It was Harry Timmons. "You going to the airport?"

"What airport?" Gammon said.

"LaGuardia."

"That where he's coming in?"

"God only knows where he's coming in. Or even if."

"Then what's the question for?"

"Because," Timmons said, "if you're going to LaGuardia, here's what you do. Jump a cab and get down to the Port Authority Building. You know where it is? Between Fifteenth and Sixteenth and between Eighth and Ninth. The big building. Whole block. You know."

"I know where it is," Gammon said.

"All right," Timmons said. "Go the Sixteenth Street side. All you've got to do is show them your press card. They've got Police and PA helicopters leaving from the roof."

"Helicopters leaving from the roof? What is this?"

"It's the word, buster, that's what it is. That's how we get it."

"No taxicabs driving to Queens tonight?"

"The taxicabs can't move any more than anybody else can. The whole city of New York is headed out to La-Guardia Field to see the show. Believe it or the marching

Chinese, like Bugs Baer says. Traffic backed up off the Triborough. Tunnel jammed. Queensboro Bridge—both levels—nobody can get on it. Astoria Boulevard and the Parkway in Queens jammed up halfway to Jones Beach. They say it's the damnedest sight in all history. Mothers sitting in the cars breast-feeding their babies. Midnight and the worst traffic jam of all time. What the hell makes sense any more?"

"Okay," Gammon said. "If I go, I go. You've got other people going, haven't you?"

"Are you kidding? Max has guys at every airport you ever heard of. Even that blimp place at Lakehurst. Remember? Where the Hindenburg blew up?"

"Okay," Gammon said again. "Thanks, Harry." He hung up the phone, then looked at Emmy. "You want to go to the airport, don't you?"

"Yes," she said, "I'd like to . . ." She stopped, and then said, "No."

"What do you mean, no?"

"I mean no."

"You don't want to go?"

"That's right."

"You'll be expected."

"What does that mean?"

"It means you'll be expected."

"By whom? Your photographers? Kissing the hero as he comes off the plane? You help that company of yours a lot on your day off, don't you? Eagle scout in person."

Gammon looked at her and said nothing.

"You don't understand," she said. For no immediate reason that Gammon could perceive, she began to cry.

"I don't know," he said. "You started out one minute by saying yes, you wanted to go, and now all of a sudden something else. No, you don't want to go."

"Why don't you quit it?" she said. She sniffed and brought her handkerchief to her eyes and nose. "I suppose I'm a sight."

"The eternal woman," Gammon said. "And on top of everything else—are you mad at me all over again?"

"No," she said. "I'm sorry. It's been a tough night for you. Hasn't it?"

"What do you mean? Hasn't it been for you?"

"Yes," she said. "But for you too."

"That's not my fiancé in that airplane."

"He's going to be all right now," she said.

"If you believe that, why don't you want to go to the airport?"

Emmy said, "I don't know."

"Don't you want to find out if he's all right?"

"Yes. Of course I do."

"Well, you make no damn sense at all," he said.

"Oh," she said, in a very small voice, a voice that was at once both frightened and somehow pleased. Then, more strongly: "Say that again."

He looked at her. "You make no sense at all."

"Now you're talking like Ben," she said. "Like my Ben."

His heart leaped. "Your Ben?"

"My Ben," she said. "All night long you've been trying to be nice. Trying; genuinely trying. That's what I meant when I said it's been a tough night for you. Being genuinely the kind of nice that doesn't come easily to you. Not like a martyr. Just nice."

Gammon said, "What happens if the plane crashes now?"

"I don't know," Emmy said, but she said it in a way to indicate she knew it was not going to crash.

Gammon stared at her for a time. Then he nodded his head slowly and went to the hall closet and got his hat down off the shelf.

"What are you going to do?" Emmy said. "I told you I didn't want to go to the airport."

"The hell with you, lady," Gammon said to her. "I don't care where you're going and I don't know where I'm going. It's the story of my life. Of all the women I've got to pick to fall in love with—"

"Ben," Emmy said.

—"it had to be somebody who'd sit and pick me apart while the other man in her life was getting ready to live or die, he wasn't sure which." He opened the front door to the apartment. "You die in more ways than one, lady. There are fifty-five different ways you can die. Sometimes you walk around for years afterwards like a goddam zombie." He nodded. "Thanks for the meat loaf."

The door closed behind him.

Emmy said, "Ben . . ."

IN PORTLAND, OREGON, the Rev. Wally Hare, greatest of the mass gospel preachers of our time, gripped the microphone before him and stared blue-eyed at the giant throng in the auditorium.

"Now, brothers and sisters, I will talk to you about the love of God tonight," he said, "and you will listen and I will pray and you will pray and we will pray together, because tonight there is an airplane in the sky, and the innocents of this world, the children, fly that plane as well as the adult brothers and sisters of us all. Say *amen*, brothers and sisters, say *amen!*"

And the word rumbled forth to him from the dark arena, for everyone there knew.

"The evil that men do lives after them," Hare intoned. "The inventions of man and the evil of man are an equation, not because the inspiration is not great, leading to these inventions, but because the evil is equally great! Amen!"

"Amen!" murmured the hall.

"Man invented the radio, and the evil in man has betrayed our brother in the sky!"

"Amen!"

"Man invented the electric light, and the evil in man has betrayed our brother in the sky!"

"Amen!"

"And do we turn to God at this late time—when perhaps it is even too late—and do we say *save them?* Only in one fashion, brothers and sisters, and that fashion is that we pray now for souls other than our own!"

"Amen!"

"For in praying for souls other than our own, only then do we pray for our own souls!"

"Amen!"

"No, there are no atheists in foxholes, brothers and sisters, because any man in danger of his own life can pray to God. What does he lose? And yet what does he prove by this?"

"Amen!"

"Pray for someone else, brothers and sisters, and thereby pray for yourselves!"

"Amen!"

"Pray for the God as certainly in the skies as our brothers and sisters beset by evil are in the sky tonight!"

"Amen!"

"A Psalm of David," Hare said. " 'O Lord our Lord, how excellent is thy name in all the earth! who hast set thy glory above the heavens.

" 'Out of the mouth of babes and sucklings hast thou ordained strength because of thine enemies, that thou mightest still the enemy and the avenger.

" 'When I consider thy heavens, the work of thy fingers, the moon and the stars, which thou hast ordained;

" 'What is man, that thou art mindful of him? and the son of man, that thou visitest him?

" 'For thou hast made him a little lower than the angels, and hast crowned him with glory and honour.

" 'Thou madest him to have dominion over the works of thy hands; thou hast put all things under his feet:

" 'All sheep and oxen, yea, and the beasts of the field;

" 'The fowl of the air, and the fish of the sea, and whatsoever passeth through the paths of the seas.

" 'O Lord our Lord, how excellent is thy name in all the earth!' "

Here and there in the hall, there came the sound of weeping.

"Obadiah," Hare said. " 'But thou shouldest not have looked on the day of thy brother in the day that he became a stranger; neither shouldest thou have rejoiced over the children of Judah in the day of their destruction; neither shouldest thou have spoken proudly in the day of distress. . . . For the day of the LORD is near upon all the heathen: as thou hast done, it shall be done unto thee: thy reward shall return upon thine own head.' "

M<small>R. KRAMER</small>! Message!" The man at the headset in the control tower at LaGuardia almost shouted the words.

"Keep your voice down," Kramer snapped. "What is it?"

"Identification, sir! The S.S. *United States!*"

"Where is she?"

"Laying off Ambrose for the night. Coming in in the morning."

"What does she say?"

"Four-engine aircraft without lights. Under the clouds at fourteen hundred feet."

"All right!" Kramer snapped.

"Message!" another man in the tower broke in. "Fort Hamilton reports recognition. Heading northbound over Sheepshead Bay!"

"Message!" the first man said. "Fort Tilden! Two searchlights have the aircraft, sir!"

"North over Sheepshead?" Kramer said.

"Estimated over the Belt Parkway at Sheepshead Bay in *two* minutes, sir!"

Kramer turned to Joe Donaldson. "Turn on your green spot."

"He's coming here, isn't he?" Donaldson said.

"Damn right," Kramer said.

"Want the other runway lit? So he doesn't have to turn?"

It was a lightning decision, but it had to be made. Coastal 214 was now maybe *eight* minutes away.

"No," Kramer said. "He knows this airport. We've got other craft to land. The less we confuse him the better off we are, and we can't afford to confuse the others. His maneuverability isn't in question. Let him make a left turn and land on the runway that's already lit up. Send downstairs and get a blinker going. Give him the runway in blinker code."

"What if he doesn't read blinker code?"

"Let it blink at him anyway."

"Want us to find him with a searchlight?"

"No. He's probably blinded enough already. Your sweep is all you need."

"Right," Donaldson said.

Kramer stepped to the middle man among the three control microphone men—one of them in contact with ATC beyond tower range; the middle one controlling take-offs and landings; the third one controlling traffic on the ground. "Who've you got, Phil?" he said to the man.

"Three planes headed by TWA 513, held short of the runway," Phil said. "Three planes to land."

"Three?"

"The third one's over Maspeth now. Here are the cards."

Kramer riffled through the cards and nodded quickly. "All right, carry on."

"TWA 513," Phil said into the microphone, "you're held where you are."

The voice in his ear, as he put on the headset, said, "513."

Phil scanned the rainy sky. "United 72, you're on final approach and cleared. Wind negligible, under twelve. American 818, you're behind that United DC-6 and cleared for final approach. Make your left turn just back of the el tracks there."

"72," the headset said to him, and, "818."

"Northwest 412," Phil said, checking with the cards that were slotted before him like time-punch cards in a factory, "you're number three to land. Can you see that Convair up ahead of you?"

"412," the headset said. "I see him."

"There's a United DC-6 making his final descent now over Flushing Bay," Phil said.

"Confirming number three to land behind the DC-6 and the Convair," the headset said. "This is Northwest 412."

"Where'd you break through?" Phil said. "I'm asking 412."

"Lower Bay at twenty-one hundred feet," 412 said.

"Now, Capital 22," Phil said, noting the next plane scheduled to land, "do you read this? This is LaGuardia Tower."

"22," a voice said.

"Are you under the clouds, 22?"

"Under the clouds at nineteen hundred, over Flatbush."

"22, hold present altitude and continue to New Rochelle, then make a left turn and fly for five miles. You're number one in the stack. That Coastal 214 will be behind you but coming down."

"22," the voice said. "Permission to ascend as much as one thousand feet?"

Phil calculated rapidly. "Permission denied. There'll be a Boston aircraft entering that stack over you. Hold your present altitude. You're ahead of that Coastal plane."

"22," the voice said.

"LaGuardia," a voice said, "this is Northeast 117, now at three thousand coming into New Rochelle."

"Make a right turn, 117," Phil said. "And hold at three thousand, following the stack pattern. You're in our stack."

"117," the voice said.

"Message!" a voice behind Phil said. "Prospect Park Signal Corps searchlight has Coastal 214."

Phil nodded. "United 72, turn off that runway at the first set of lights."

"72," the headset said.

"American 818, you're cleared for final approach," Phil said.

"818."

"Eastern 92, is your altitude over four thousand?"

"Eastern 92. Just about at four thousand. Still in cloud."

"Fly for one minute and make a left turn," Phil said. "Then you'll be flying north toward New Rochelle. You'll be number three in the stack."

"92."

"Northwest 412, I can see you making your turn."

"Over Flushing Meadow, this is 412."

"You're back of that Convair."

"Right. 412."

"American 623," Phil said, "you're held back of that TWA Constellation on the ground. All departing traffic is held where it is awaiting clearance."

"623."

"Northwest 412," Phil said. "The wind is negligible. You are now cleared for final approach."

"412."

"He's the last to land," Joe Donaldson said, standing at Kramer's elbow.

"Message!" snapped a voice behind them. "Coastal 214 reported headed directly for airport at one thousand feet, headed northbound!"

Donaldson's eyes grew large. "He can't! Wrong runway! That runway's not lit! Can't he see?"

"Sure he can see," Kramer said.

"Then what's he doing? How can he . . . ?"

"Listen," Kramer said.

Donaldson listened. From outside there came dimly the

din as if from the throats of a thousand frogs. It was louder than that, of course. A portable Army searchlight truck, rolled into position at the Marine fringe of LaGuardia, fingered its light through the glistening rain toward the south.

The noise came from thousands of automobile horns.

The people had seen it.

Then almost immediately, in the bright wet green of the vertical spot, a four-engine aircraft flew directly over the tower, no more than nine hundred feet high.

Underneath one black-wet wing in the darkness, the green light picked out the one word:

C O A S T A L.

"Just buzzing us," Kramer said. "Letting us know who he is."

"Listen to those horns, will you?" Donaldson said. "What's he going to do now? Right turn?"

"Theoretically he ought only to right-turn with permission," Kramer said.

"If he turns left he's got to turn the corner three times."

"Watch him," Kramer said. "Where is he? Do you still see him?"

"Heading for the five stacks," Donaldson said. "See the light? There."

"I bet he's a busy fella looking around him right about now," Kramer said. "Although you'd think he'd realize from the green light that the way was clear."

"Can't be too sure," Donaldson said. "There. He *is* turning left."

"Are his wheels down? I can't see?"

"He's got a buzzer in there that'll remind him if they're not," Donaldson said.

"Perhaps the most minor thing of all," Kramer said, "but, Joe, just as certain as anything else that isn't working in that plane, that buzzer isn't."

"I forgot," Donaldson said. "Well, do you think he'll remember?"

"I think so," Kramer said. "Is your crash equipment set?"

"You can see 'em," Donaldson said. "Either side of the runway. Fire, ambulance, the works." He grinned tensely. "Even a couple of people from the CAA."

"I want that airplane taken right to that hangar," Kramer said. "We're going to lock it up overnight. Is all that set?"

"Yes," Donaldson said. "You know, Lou, wouldn't it be something if after everything he went through he crashed it coming down?"

"Where is he?" Kramer asked. "Is that him?"

"Over Astoria," Donaldson said. "See him in that light?"

Kramer nodded. "You got a line to that Army truck?"

"I don't know. I think so."

"Tell them to cut that light."

"What for?" Donaldson said. "You going to lose him now?"

"If anything's going to go wrong with him now," Kramer said, "that searchlight won't stop it. Meanwhile, coming around that final bend, it'll be in his eyes."

Donaldson said to one of the men on the phones behind him, "You hear that? Get that light cut."

"Now all aircraft," Phil said into the microphone, "hold your altitudes. Eastern 92, fly north for two more minutes and make a left turn."

"92," the headset said.

"Informatively we have that Coastal aircraft on a final approach pattern," Phil said into the microphone.

"He's coming up the el tracks now," Donaldson said. "See him?"

"*Get that light off!*" Kramer snapped. "*Get it off!*"

"Now he's turning," Donaldson said. "I can't see his wheels, Lou. I can't see his wheels! Put your wheels down, damn it, put your wheels down!"

"Five more degrees and that light will be dead into his eyes," Kramer said. "I want that light off or I'm going to find out why!"

"His wheels . . ." Donaldson said.

"What about them?"

"You can't see them. He must have forgot . . . Look for yourself, in the light."

Kramer looked, and as he did so the searchlight from the far end of the field went out.

In the after-effect of the light, no one looking out from the tower could see a thing, for the night was suddenly black upon black, and the sound of the automobile horns and, a little closer, the rain itself joined in a weird cacophony that seemed to isolate those in the tower completely.

"TWA 513," Phil said into the microphone, talking to the Constellation that was now awaiting clearance for take-off just beside the end of the runway. "That dark aircraft is on final descent, over the water by now, I think. Will you watch for him?"

"What do you think I'm doing?" the headset said, not in the least bit disrespectfully.

The tower fell into silence.

With the deadening of the searchlight, the noise of the automobile horns had quickly died down; now it was hardly noticeable.

Even the rain seemed far away.

Kramer switched on the loud-speaker system, already dialed to Phil's wave length, so everyone in the tower could hear. An emergency now would require action by more than one man in the control area, and the news of it would come from the Constellation on Phil's wave length, most likely.

The sound of restive static, like an ocean tide, in the tower now.

Kramer looked at the clock:

1:17 A.M.

1:17 A.M. and 13 seconds. 14. 15. 16.

To the east, the bay and the sky black and impenetrable. Runway lights to the water's edge, and beside them the blinking wing and tail lights of the patient TWA Connie and the two other waiting aircraft behind it.

"All craft in the sky, radio silence please," Phil said into the microphone. Every plane in the stack was listening, he knew, waiting . . .

1:17 A.M. and 22 seconds. 23. 24.

The pulsing red lights of emergency truck after emergency truck winked flanking both sides of the runway.

Joe Donaldson said to himself, "*The wheels . . . I didn't see the wheels . . .*"

Blackness, rain, and the second hand of the clock.

1:17 A.M. and 28 seconds. 29.

And a voice!

"Tower, that plane's . . ."

A pause. A pause for how long? Half a second? A full second? More . . . ?

". . . down and . . ."

And *what?*

". . . now landed smoothly. This is 513. He's already

past that first emergency equipment. He's reversing engines, I think, we hear him clearly . . ."

Louis Kramer put his hand against his eyes and stood there for a moment. He heard Phil saying into the microphone, "Now this is tower, we've been on radio silence but that dark plane is safely in. Trans-Canada 51 and Mohawk 312, please report your positions in order. We believe we can see you both . . ."

Kramer looked out the window and saw a grease monkey perched on a fire truck with a green guide flash in his hand, turning the Everyinch off the runway . . .

FIRST OFF THE PLANE had been the newlyweds, Mr. and Mrs. James Laurie of Brooklyn, New York, and their in-laws were there to meet them. Back of the police lines surrounding the front of the hangar where the Everyinch had pulled up, the public pushed and thronged and strained to see.

"We weren't worried for a minute," Mr. Laurie choked. "Believe me."

"Worried about what?" his son asked him.

"He was the one who was worried," Mr. Laurie said, and leveled a finger at Mr. Kramer.

"I was worried for a minute, that's all," Mr. Kramer said. "Then I stopped worrying. You know why? We found out the head man in the whole system here upstairs in that glass window there is named Kramer. His name is Louis Kramer! A relative! You know who he is? A cousin of your cousin Sidney; Lena, what do you think of that?"

"What were you worrying about?" the bride asked.

The Diaz family came off the plane next. The woman was holding her baby, and the husband had the other two boys by the hand. They looked around and saw the entire outskirts of the field jammed with thousands of people as the photographers engulfed them. Their relatives were nowhere to be seen, still trapped as they were in the traffic on the Triborough Bridge.

"We sent a telegram," Rafael Diaz said, looking around him. "But no one is here."

"First trip to the United States?" a reporter asked.

"Yes," Rafael Diaz said.

"You talk good English."

"Thank you, sir."

"How was the trip?"

"We were delayed. By winds, I believe."

"Didn't you notice the lights were out?"

"They were not working. The hostess explained this to everyone."

"Were you scared?"

"Scared?"

"Afraid."

"Of what? Where are my relatives? They were supposed to be here, along with several of their companions."

"You must have known *something* was wrong," the reporter said.

"I have told you the lights went out early in the journey," Rafael Diaz said. "We will have to go to—" he disengaged the hand of his older boy and reached in his pocket for a piece of paper, to read the address written there—"six-two-seven east one hundred eighteenth street. Please, where is the bus?"

"You leave from here by helicopter," the reporter said. "Meanwhile, what did . . ."

"You hear that?" Diaz said to his wife. "Helicopter. Is it not a fabulous country?"

Mrs. Albie Webber and her daughter came off the plane next. Albie Webber, the fighter, was waiting there to embrace them, and Hatsky Gideon, the puncho bodyguard, swept the little girl into his arms and said, "It was a unanimous knockout in the first round. You understand?"

Mrs. Webber heard what Hatsky said. She said to her husband, "Albie, did you really win?"

"Big," he said in a broken voice. "Big, honey. Next we go for the title."

"I asked the stewardess three times to find out from the pilot on his radio how it came out," Mrs. Webber said, "but she said it was against company regulations, and I told her about that other time I flew on United and *they* got me the result of the fight that time, but she still wouldn't do it, and the lights were off on the plane the whole trip and . . . well, you don't know how hard I was praying for you."

Mrs. K. L. Sherman came off the plane, with a thin, neutral-looking man behind her. Mr. Sherman was waiting there. He was crying again. "Dorothy," he wept. "Oh, Dorothy, Dorothy."

"Bastard," his wife said to him in a low voice, averting her mouth from his. "You want to pay him off now or later?"

"Pay him off?" Mr. Sherman said, his voice equally low, and he looked fearfully around.

"The clown," Mrs. Sherman said, straightening her shoulders underneath the mink stole she wore and gesturing with her head toward the man who had come off the plane behind her. "The detective you had follow me all over Miami for ten days. Your buddy. John Black, he says his name is. Go ahead. Ask him what he found out."

"I'm so happy you're alive, Dorothy," Sherman said.

"I'm not," Dorothy Sherman said.

Herman Jonas of Miami, Florida, came off the plane, and they made way for him understandingly when he said he wanted to call his home long distance. He called and spoke to his wife to assure her he was all right—having slept up to and including the landing, he did not know he might not have been all right till the newspapermen told him. Then he said hello to his stepson.

"I'm glad you're all right," the boy said to him. Was his voice unusually strained and distant, or was it merely the phone connection?

"You can call me Dad, Andrew," Herman Jonas said to him. "Yes, I'm fine."

"That's nice," Andrew said. "Dad." There was a pause. Then the boy said, "I hope you weren't frightened?"

"I am now," Herman Jonas said, and giggled into the telephone. "But we weren't during the trip. It was a very smooth trip, really."

"Then you'll keep only flying when you travel?" the boy said.

"Oh, by all means," Herman Jonas said. "Did you call me Dad?"

"Dad."

"Isn't that wonderful?" Jonas said. "Now, you tell me, Andrew. Is there anything I can get you while I'm here in New York? You know your old dad wants to do right by you."

"Well," the boy said, "there is one thing. Dad. You can't get one in Miami, but there's a place called Wenning's in New York . . ."

"Wenning's?"

"That's right," the boy said, and spelled it out. "Scientific equipment. A specialty house. What I need isn't too expensive."

"Don't you worry about money," Jonas said to him.

"Thank you, Dad," the boy said. "It's called a Gomburg reactor."

"A Gomburg reactor," Jonas said. "Now, just let me write that down. A Gomburg reactor."

"It's for one of my new inventions," the boy said.

"I didn't know you were working on a new invention," Jonas said.

"Oh, yes," the boy said. "It's almost finished."

"I'd love to see it."

"I hope to have it ready before your next trip."

"That would be marvelous," Jonas said.

"Yes, Dad," the boy said.

And finally came the crew of Coastal 214.

The flight engineer, to find his father there waiting— the co-pilot and stewardess, to call their homes long-distance—these alone realizing what the danger had been.

And last, Mike Trace, the pilot.

The newspapermen had his ex-wife, Karen, up on the top step of the ramp to meet him.

The television cameras went live under the klieg lights.

Across the nation, fifty million people saw it.

Karen threw her arms around Mike and kissed him.

"Well," he said. "Well. This is a surprise."

"It must have been horrible, darling," his ex-wife said to him. She talked loudly enough for the pickup microphone that Mike Trace did not realize was there. It was 12:30 A.M. in Chicago, 11:30 P.M. in Phoenix, 10:30 P.M. in Los Angeles. All three networks had this on camera. A nation watched and listened.

Mike Trace, knowing none of this, recalled none the less how fresh and warm and delicious Karen was. And the strange thing was, he had been through tougher flights than this: had had an engine quit on take-off once in the Azores, had had a wheel buckle on landing at Fort Worth. Here he had known they could see him on radar, and he had come down under the clouds several times to check his position. He had ridden the last stretch into New York well under the customary altitude, and the result was he could not have hit another plane if he'd tried. The last half of the trip, the ceiling had stayed high enough so he could descend under the clouds and still be seen on close-range radar. The only really tough part had been the beginning, and then only for a short space in time—the proper decision not to turn back to Miami; and the part of the trip well over the ocean where, distrusting his star fix, he had come down so close to the water to learn where he was. But that had worked out fine. He recognized Hatteras and the mainland to the left, and from that point on he knew he was all right. His wrist watch told him at that point that his fuel reserves would be there. From then on, there was no question in his mind, even though Ken Belding, the co-pilot, had said it was no better than 60–40 some————jet would come out and shoot the bejesus out of them.

Marv Goldstone, the engineer-navigator, had even insisted that somebody down there in the rain on that desolate Ocracoke Island, just south of Hatteras, was actually shining a flashlight up at the plane. How crazy could you get?

Yet here was a mob of people such as Mike Trace had never seen, and flashbulbs, and—what was that?—a television camera atop a truck?

"I know what you went through," Karen Trace said to him. "You're the only man I've ever loved. How can I make it up to you?"

Mike Trace told her how she could make it up to him. The positioning of the microphone boom being what it was, fifty million Americans, including the preacher in Oregon, learned his opinion of how she could make it up to him.

They brought the portable kennel crate into the cargo office of the airline, and Mrs. Cameron Fletcher III was there to liberate her dog, Champion Venerable Lady Standaright of Locust Farm.

"Boo-boo," she said, crying. "It's me. Mother."

"I'm a son-of-a-bitch," Harrison, the Coastal Cargo man, said as he watched the animal come snarling out of the cage toward her mistress. "She *does* bite."

In the Operations Room, Vice-President Marshall Kent of Coastal Airlines said to Willard Trace, "So. You're the one who called out the news."

"I called my brother's girl," Willard said stiffly.

"You mean the one kissing him on the ladder out there?"

"No," Willard said. "That's the woman he married. I mean his girl."

"You're fired," Kent said to him.

"Thank you," Willard Trace said.

Kent looked at him. "What do you mean, 'thank you'?"

"I mean I'm glad you said that," Willard said. "Because I don't like you, Mr. Kent. I'm glad I'm not working for you any more. That's all I meant. Most of the big men in this airline are wonderful men, but you make up for all of them all by yourself."

"Oh," Kent said, and nodded heavily. "Idiot gets fired, so he comes back with the speech about the nasty old boss. That's happened before, too. If you felt that way, why didn't you ever quit?"

"I never felt that way till tonight," Willard Trace said.

"Well, while you're at it, think about something else, too," Kent said to him. "And that is that you haven't heard the end of this from me. Informing the newspapers was . . ."

"Mr. Kent?"

It was a voice at the door of the room, and Kent wheeled to see who it was.

The newcomer came in the door. "My name is Max Wild. I'm general manager of the Global Press Association."

"Ah, yes," Kent said. "I hope you're pleased with your little scoop, Mr. Wild. You were the first of them, weren't you? You were out ahead with the news. You had all those phony lines about ghost planes and planes that were supposed to have crashed. You caused the biggest automobile traffic jam they ever had around here. You and your sensational yellow journalism. Don't ever bother with any facts. Just get headlines, that's all. Can you stand there and wonder why you don't get any more co-operation than you do? When you act the way you act, you get what you deserve." Kent's face was red. "You know what this was tonight? A routine flight. Trouble, yes. But it didn't endanger a man, woman, or child. You realize that? After all your shrieking and shouting all over the country, you realize it?"

"I wouldn't call it routine," Wild said in a quiet voice.

"Let's say it was a safe flight," Kent said. "In our business, safe flights and routine flights are one and the same thing, but maybe you don't understand that. Maybe you talk a different language. All right. Let's just say it was a safe flight. You admit that?"

"Yes. Do you know why it was safe?"

"Of course I know. You don't, though."

"No?" Wild said.

"No," Kent said.

"It was safe," Wild said, "because the people found out about it."

Kent stared at him. "What people?"

"Just people," Max Wild said. "People everywhere. There were people that prayed for that airplane tonight, Mr. Kent. Do you know that?"

"Wait till I get my violin," Marshall Kent said to him. "Meanwhile, were any of your lovely people doing anything else except praying? Was there anything else, anything maybe a little more direct, that they could do?"

"At least one other thing that I know of," Wild said.

"I'm listening."

"That Ground Observer Corps man on Hatteras."

"Oh, sure." Kent laughed. "Big hero. Hero of the night."

"No," Wild said, "the hero of the night isn't this man. This man heard about the plane on the radio. The hero of the night is a newspaperman. He works for me. Name is Ben Gammon."

"I talked to him on the phone," Kent said.

Wild nodded. "It was his day off, and he was in a situation where he might have thought a lot differently than he did. But the one way he thought was to call his office. That's what started it. A very small thing, Mr. Kent, but that's what touched it off."

"That must be significant to your way of thinking," Kent said.

"It is," Max Wild said.

"So?"

"So, as a result of the bulletin he heard on the radio, this old man on Hatteras identified your airplane."

"Big deal," Kent said. "Big, big deal. And three minutes later twenty radar screens had him back on there and made the same identification."

"Yes," Max Wild said, "but that man standing there in the rain on Cape Hatteras told you the one thing you had to know to *make* it a safe flight. The one thing the radar couldn't tell you."

"Oh really?"

"Yes, oh really."

"And what was that?"

"He told you what to look for."

"I got a little news for you," Kent said. "Every man on the searchlights, every man in the tower here, every man connected with the last stages of that flight, knew what to look for. They didn't need a nut on Cape Hatteras to tell them the plane's license number or markings or shape or anything else. We knew. And in the last stages of the flight, it wasn't a nut on Cape Hatteras telling us what to look for. We had that plane pegged all the way. What did your man tell us that the radar didn't?"

"He told you what to look for," Max Wild said again patiently. "So searchlights could pick him out in the sky and let him know for certain he was expected at his landing field."

Kent said, "I don't get this. Radar told us what we had to know."

"No," Wild said. "Radar merely said the plane is there, and if you'd looked for it there was a chance you might have missed it—could have lost precious time before you found it in that black sky, anyway—because all radar said was look for a plane."

"All right," Kent said, exasperated, "so all radar said was look for a plane. That's all that man said, too."

"No," Max Wild said gently. "That man said look for a plane without lights."

A<small>T TWO O'CLOCK</small> in the morning, Ben Gammon rang Emmy's doorbell. She answered it, still fully dressed. She had been watching the airport scene—including the part with Mike Trace and Karen—on television.

"I'm sorry, lady," Ben said to Emmy. "That's all. I just came to say I'm sorry."

She said nothing, only stood there looking at him, so he said, "I mean for what I said to you. That's all."

"Ben?" she said in a soft voice.

"Ayuh, I've been drinking," he said, "if that's what you want to know. But I'm not stiff. I will be before the night's over, but I'm not now. I just came to apologize. That's the whole thing together."

"Stop saying that's all," she said to him, "and come in here."

He looked at her uncertainly. "Come in here?"

"Yes. Please."

"And then what?"

"And then you can kiss me."

"Like the flyboy kissed the blonde coming off the plane?" Gammon said. "I watched it on television in Horatio's bar and grill below. You know what I think? I think the whole thing was an act. From the minute he took off from Miami. The clinch at the end with the ex-wife. Here is the hunter, home from the hill, and the sailor home from the . . ." He stared at her, still standing in the doorway. "And that's why you didn't want to go to the airport. You couldn't very well share the spotlight with an ex-wife. Very smart." He tapped himself on the temple, then nodded. "And I was feeling sorry because of you."

Emmy laughed.

"Quit it," he said uncertainly. "What's funny?"

"Come in, Algernon Charles," she said. "That's it. Come on. Give me that wet hat of yours." She steered him into the apartment.

"Now what?" he said.

"Now the lady tells the man she loves him," Emmy said, "and loved him before tonight, but didn't find out till now."

"Oh," Gammon said quietly; then, more loudly: "Oh." He thought for a moment. "What for?"

"Because he's just her Bill," Emmy said.

ALL ALONE in his New York apartment, Felix Allerdyce, the advertising man, reflected that his firm might well still land the Coastal Airlines account. It would be well not to press it for a few days, but it was going to be all right, he felt sure.

After all, there was the marvelous slogan that he himself had coined. And marvelous was not too strong a word for it. It had all the necessary elements—it embodied a familiar phrase, one that was easy to remember, one that could bear the repetition necessary to put a new slogan across with the public. As for subject matter, it played up the airlines' greatest advantage—speed—without intruding the stubborn fact that frequently ground transportation or air traffic or weather difficulties of one kind and another slowed the passengers down. This slogan stressed the element of speed without committing the airline to timetable accuracy.

What with the excitement tonight, not to mention Marshall Kent's neuralgia or whatever it was, Allerdyce had not had the chance to show the slogan to the Coastal vice-president.

Now, though, he took out the large Manila folder from his desk drawer and extracted the beautifully lettered slogan, inked on a great square of white vellum underneath the handsome picture of a Coastal Airlines plane in flight.

The slogan said:

> *Be There*
> *in*
> *No Time at All*

And Felix Allerdyce smiled and replaced the slogan in its envelope and had a small drink of excellent brandy and went to bed and had a rather disquieting dream in which somebody kept repeating the clincher on the slogan—No Time at All—No Time at All—while, in dreadful counterpoint, somebody else kept chanting, "The Miles Never Show . . ."

ABOUT THE AUTHOR

Born in Boston in 1926, Charles Einstein went through New York City public schools and then on to Horace Mann, but moved west for his college education and took his degree at the age of 19 from the University of Chicago. Since then he has resided for the greater part in the New York area, but recently he has picked up his wife and four children and moved them to a desert mountain home in Scottsdale, Arizona.

Einstein has been a sports writer, Midwest sports editor, and assistant sports editor for the International News Service, with whom he went after leaving college, and stayed until late 1953. He resigned then to become a full-time free-lance writer, and his short stories and articles have been appearing ever since in practically every major magazine. In addition he has written several novels, was the co-author with Willie Mays of the latter's autobiography, and has edited The Fireside Book of Baseball.